THE BEVERLY GRAY
MYSTERY STORIES

Beverly Gray, Senior

The BEVERLY GRAY *Mystery Stories*

By CLAIR BLANK

BEVERLY GRAY
SENIOR

By CLAIR BLANK

GROSSET & DUNLAP
Publishers   NEW YORK

Copyright, 1934, by
GROSSET & DUNLAP INC.

Beverly Gray, Senior
PRINTED IN THE UNITED STATES OF AMERICA

CONTENTS

Contents

CHAPTER I

Seniors

"FOR IT'S ALWAYS fair weather when good Alphas get together——" sang Lois Mason loudly and enthusiastically.

"Except when one particular Alpha insists on giving voice to her feelings," commented Lenora Whitehill dryly.

"At least they are jolly feelings," her friend replied saucily.

"When do you suppose they will arrive?" Shirley Parker asked for the tenth time, leaning halfway out the window in her impatience.

"The train is due at three," Rosalie Arnold answered. "It is five of three now."

"Preserve your soul in patience," Lenora begged the irritable Shirley. "Our estimable class president and her companion will arrive in good time."

"We should have gone to the station to meet them," Lois declared. "But Lenora had the crazy idea that it would be fun to surprise them here."

"It isn't a crazy idea," Lenora defended. "I distinctly like to be comfortable when waiting for anyone." She demonstrated this statement by depositing herself cozily in a nest of cushions. "And who, might I ask, can be comfortable on one of the rickety wooden benches in the railway station?"

"If they don't come soon I shall go down to the station anyway," Shirley declared.

"And spoil our surprise?" wailed Lenora. "The ice cream will all melt away, and the cake——"

"Lenora will eat the cake," put in Lois, "if we leave her alone with it for five minutes."

"And she insists she is losing weight," added Rosalie.

"Yes," Lois said frowning on Lenora, "my friend, you are slightly inclined to plumpness."

"I am not," Lenora defended. "I shan't forget that slighting remark," she vowed. "Remember, it is said that elephants and women never forget!"

"Now, we didn't say you look like an elephant," soothed Shirley.

"You better not," declared Lenora. "Something tells me that I am getting the worst of this argument."

"What wonderful powers of deduction!" murmured Lois.

The four girls were gathered in one of the dormitory rooms in Chadwick Hall awaiting the arrival of two more of their members, Beverly Gray and Anne White. The latter two were on their way from their home town of Renville back to Vernon. The other girls had arrived earlier in the day and gathered to surprise Beverly and Anne.

Previous readers are already acquainted with the six Alpha Deltas of Vernon College. If you have followed the adventures of the girls through *Beverly Gray, Freshman, Sophomore,* and *Junior,* you know that Lois Mason and Lenora Whitehill are considered the two madcaps of the class and that they share rooms respectively with Anne and Rosalie. Former readers are also acquainted with Beverly Gray and her roommate, Shirley Parker, the girl who had started her college life in such an unfortunate manner but who, with Beverly's help, had developed into the sunny, cheerful girl that she now is. The girls had organized into a club in their sophomore year and they had proved themselves a moving light in the events of college life. They were known far and wide on the campus as the six chums who stood firmly by one another in rain or shine, in mischievous or noble acts.

"Here they come," Shirley cried jubilantly. "They are just rounding the driveway."

"Goody, goody," squealed Lois.

"Come on, girls, hide," Lenora directed. "When

Beverly opens the door we will all promptly jump out and besiege them."

Lois and Rosalie disappeared into the closet while Lenora dived behind a desk and Shirley stepped behind the door. For several seconds total silence reigned in the room. Gay voices could be heard in the hall, calling back and forth. Two girls, laden with suitcases and tennis racquets, answered the gleeful hails with laughs and cheery words, until they stopped before the room upon which silence had so lately descended.

"I wonder why the Alphas didn't meet us," Anne murmured. "Perhaps none of them are back yet."

"Perhaps not," Beverly agreed and swung open the door.

Immediately the air was rent with wild shouts of "Surprise! Surprise!" and the two slender, suntanned travelers were besieged by delighted, ecstatic arms.

"Were you disappointed when we didn't meet you?" demanded Lenora after the noise of greeting had died down.

"Terribly," Beverly declared laughing. "When did you get back?"

"This morning," Shirley answered.

"Yep," continued Lois, "we are all settled already."

"And we thought we would have a surprise party for you," Rosalie added.

"Splendid!" declared Beverly.

"With ice cream and everything," Lenora informed them.

"Lead us to it," begged Anne. "I can hardly wait."

"Is everybody back?" Beverly asked, as the girls devoured the ice cream and delicious little cakes.

"Yes," Lenora informed her, "everybody is back, and it promises to be a most momentous term!"

"Ah, that sounds interesting," Beverly declared. "Is there a mystery in the air?"

"No," Lois answered, "but Connie Elwood and her gang are back in full bloom."

"That means a headache for us," continued Lenora. "Those juniors are out to rival the Alphas in popularity."

"Personally, Connie gives me a pain," Shirley said frowning. "I violently dislike that girl."

"Why?" Beverly asked wonderingly. "Did she do something to you?"

"No," Shirley answered.

"She and her pals can think up more mischief than any six girls I know," Anne declared.

"What?" Lois demanded indignantly. "Are you forgetting our noble organization? We've always kept things moving."

"We're seniors now," Rosalie reminded them, "and we have to behave."

"We are only here for a short while, anyhow," continued Anne, "and we want to leave pleasant memories behind us."

"Will you please stop reminding me that we have to leave soon?" Lenora grumbled. "I don't see why you have to rub it in. It is going to be hard enough without anticipating it 'way ahead of time."

"Forget I said anything," Rosalie interrupted.

"Just the same," Lois continued, "we can't let Connie and her crowd run things on the campus."

"What with the Forsythe Film Company making a moving picture right here on the campus, and Connie and her friends, the term promises to be most exciting," Beverly said.

"Don't forget your duties as president of the graduating class," Shirley reminded her friend. "You will, at least, be busy."

"You're telling me," Beverly returned slangily. "I'm already planning my speech for commencement."

"Another thing," continued Lois, "we heard that the faculty is thinking of running all the campus houses on the Student Control basis."

"What's that?" Anne asked.

"Previously there has been a teacher on every

floor of the Hall to keep peace in the rooms," explained Lois. "Now the teachers are to leave and things are going to be put in the hands of an upper classman."

"Some fun," murmured Lenora. "I wonder how many girls will listen to an upper classman? They obeyed the teachers because they were afraid of them, but another student——"

"It won't work," agreed Shirley.

"It might," declared Beverly. "If the right girl was in charge she could find means to make the other girls keep in line."

"You ought to know," said Lenora. "You are to be it."

"I'm to be what?" demanded Beverly.

"You are to be second in charge of the Hall. First Mrs. Dennis will have supreme authority, and then you."

"How do you know?" Anne asked.

"I overheard Miss Wilder and Mrs. Dennis talking at luncheon today," continued Lenora.

"Of course you listened," jeered Lois.

"Of course I did," said Lenora, unabashed. "Didn't the news concern one of the Alphas, and don't we stick together through thick and thin?"

"Then if I am to have such a responsibility, I immediately appoint each one of you as assistants."

said Beverly promptly. "That will make you be good."

"You will need assistants," declared Lois. "Connie Elwood and her junior friends will balk you at every turn."

"I hope not," said Beverly frowning.

"Fear not, fair maiden," said Lenora dramatically. "Your gallant assistants will slay the ferocious dragons!"

CHAPTER II

Six Virtues

BEVERLY assumed her duties as head of the Hall the very next day, and she and her assistants were kept busy settling difficulties among the freshmen about rooms and other difficulties among the sophomores and juniors. Connie Elwood and her friends, as had been predicted, kept Beverly and her friends on tiptoe. They found fault constantly with Beverly's management and delighted in harassing her before the lower classmen. Beverly went sublimely on her way, ignoring all Connie's tricks and attempts to quarrel. As a result, the indignation of the "outlaws," as Lenora and Lois had dubbed Connie and her henchmen, grew daily.

Besides her duties as second in charge of the Hall, Beverly was president of the graduating class, and affairs of the seniors kept her busy. The room she and Shirley shared in Chadwick Hall was becoming the most popular room in the building. At all hours of the day girls dropped in with plans or suggestions to lay before Beverly and to get her sanction on proposed activities.

Beverly was, too, a reporter on the college paper, the *Comet,* for it was her dream and desire after college days to be a writer. She hoped some day to be a correspondent on a leading newspaper, and toward this end she had joined the staff of the *Comet.* But now, with class affairs piling up and this new responsibility of the Hall on her shoulders, her newspaper work was going by without much attention. Occasionally she submitted an article to the editor, but it was not often that she had much time to write.

All the college was looking forward to the arrival of the Forsythe Film Company. Last term the film company had decided to make a picture on the college grounds, and some of the students were to be given minor rôles. As a result, each girl was preening herself for her chance before the camera and confident that she would prove a big find to the director who let her act. The money that the college received for allowing the picture people to film the real college buildings and classrooms was to go for building a new indoor swimming pool for the students.

It was three weeks after the opening of college,

and Beverly had stolen a few minutes from her activities to spend with the other Alphas in Weller's, the ice-cream saloon in Vernon, favorite of the college students.

"We hardly have a chance to talk to you any more," Shirley grumbled to Beverly.

"I almost forgot what you looked like," added Lenora.

Beverly laughed. "That will never do, I will have to give you my photograph so you can't forget me."

"You have been busy, haven't you?" Anne murmured. "Every time I see you, you are either rushing from some place or to keep an appointment with somebody else."

"What is the latest news from the senior front?" queried Lois.

"A valedictorian for graduation is being discussed," Beverly said smiling. "We have about decided to ask Shirley to——"

"Me?" Shirley cried, flushing with pleasure.

"Yes. You have a wonderful speaking voice, and you are not flustered or embarrassed when you appear before an audience," Beverly continued. "If you are asked, you will take it, won't you?"

"Will I take it?" Shirley echoed.

"We will jump on her if she doesn't," declared

Lenora. "Imagine! Valedictorian and president in our society! Whoops, my dear!"

"Will Connie Elwood bite her fingernails!" giggled Lois. "Her club will never be as popular next term as we are this term."

"Oh, well, look who we are," said Lenora modestly. "Everyone has to admit that we are good."

"My, don't we hate ourself," murmured Anne laughingly.

"Speak of the devil," whispered Lois. "Direct your gaze toward the door and behold Connie Elwood and her guardsmen."

"Kathleen Ryan, Ada Collins, Evelyn DeLong, Virginia Harris, Phyllis Tanner, and the noble Connie herself," enumerated Rosalie. "They've seen us."

The six newcomers paused for a moment at the table occupied by the six Alphas and beamed on them.

"How are the Six Virtues today?" inquired Connie laughingly.

"Never better," spoke up Lenora. "We trust you are all well?"

"Fine and rarin' to go," declared Evelyn De-Long.

"Don't go too far," begged Lois. "Chadwick Hall couldn't do without you."

"We know that," admitted Connie promptly.

"Say, Beverly, when is my window going to be fixed? Every time I try to open it the——"

"It has already been fixed," Beverly interrupted.

"See you later," Lenora said, grinning as the six moved off.

"She was all ready to hop on Beverly about that window," laughed Shirley. "Was there really something wrong with it, Beverly?"

"No," Beverly said dryly. "She has been manufacturing complaints for the last two weeks. It hasn't been fixed because there was nothing to fix, but I wanted her to save her breath."

"How do you stand for those six, Beverly?" demanded Lois. "They are always running to you with some fancied wrong. It would give me the jitters."

"It is beginning to get on my nerves too," admitted Beverly. "Some day I'll explode."

"Not you," smiled Rosalie. "You are too patient."

"They will get tired of teasing after a while," added Anne.

"Connie ought to go jump in a lake," said Shirley.

Lenora laughed. "I take it you don't like the noble Connie?"

"She is my special brand of poison," declared Shirley. "Ever since——"

"Ever since what?" encouraged Beverly.

"Oh, nothing," evaded Shirley. "What did she mean by calling us the Six Virtues?"

"Haven't you heard?" asked Lois. "We are being held up to the lower classmen as models, whether for ridicule or not I can't decide. Connie and her bunch christened us the Six Virtues."

"But what is the idea?" asked Beverly.

"Each one of us is a different virtue," explained Lenora. "Lois is Truth, because she always says what she thinks, and Rosalie is Silence. Anne is Forbearance."

"Shirley is Courtesy," continued Lois, "and Lenora is Good-Humor, while you, Beverly, are Honor."

"Do you suppose they named us those things as an insult?" asked Lenora suspiciously. "I haven't been able to quite make up my mind whether they are laughing up their sleeves at us or not."

"They might have meant it as a compliment," suggested Beverly, laughing.

"That settles it!" said Lenora promptly. "I know it is an insult now. They never complimented us in their lives."

"Give them a chance," said Anne.

"They aren't really such terrible people," added

Beverly. "I think they would be jolly fun if we knew them well."

"I know enough of them now," declared Lenora with vigor.

"And I," added Shirley. "I have no desire for a closer acquaintance."

CHAPTER III

Arrival

THE GIRLS lingered a little longer over their sodas
and then made their way out into the street. They
wandered idly along, looking in shop windows and
talking about campus news.

"What's up?" Lenora demanded.

A girl was running from the railway station
toward them.

"The film company has arrived," she shouted as
she dashed past, eager to spread the news to other
Vernon students.

"Let's go down to the station," Lois suggested.

More students were making their way to the station, where the film company's private car had
been sidetracked. The arrival of the moving-
picture people direct from Hollywood was an
event in Vernon. The new arrivals were in the nature of a curiosity to the residents of the secluded
little college town. People were pouring from the

private film car, and the girls surveyed them with
interest. Directors, actors, cameramen, all of them
descended onto the ground and regarded the little
town with distaste. It did not promise much
amusement for them.

"They don't seem pleased, do they?" Lois
giggled.

"I imagine Vernon is quite a come-down when
compared with Hollywood," murmured Rosalie.

"What did they expect to find?" demanded
Lenora. "My word!" she murmured in awe. "Who
is this grand person?"

A dazzling figure in spotless white appeared on
the car steps. The dark beauty's languid glance
roved over the scene before her with insolent boredom. The red lips, slightly redder than nature intended them to be, curled in disdain.

"I presume that is the star," Shirley murmured
haughtily, in perfect imitation of the star's pose.

"I presume you presumed right," laughed Lois.
"And there is Mr.—whatzisname."

"Forsythe," supplied Beverly.

"Hmm, the owner or manager or whatever they
call him," continued Lois. "We met him last
spring, remember?"

"Of course we do," Anne answered.

Mr. Forsythe stepped down beside the star. His
gaze, roving over the scene of busy people hurry-

ing here and there, rested on the six Alphas. He smiled engagingly. He remembered the girls as the ones the Dean had introduced to him as the most popular group on the campus.

The girls returned his smile beamingly and were thrilled when they recognized the fact that he was bringing the star over to meet them. Out of the corner of their eyes they noted the effect of this on Connie Elwood and her companions, late arrivals at the scene.

To the girls' acknowledgments of the introduction by Mr. Forsythe, the star, Marcia Lyman, condescended to smile frigidly and murmur a distinctly cold "How-do-you-do?"

"Can you girls recommend a hotel where Miss Lyman might stay?" Mr. Forsythe asked.

"The Stonecleft," Lenora said smilingly before any of the others could answer, "is very nice."

"Then we will go there," the man responded, and the two moved off.

"What possessed you to say the Stonecleft?" demanded Lois laughing. "It is the worst place in town!"

"I know it," Lenora grinned, "but she needs something like that. Let her discover how uncomfortable it is for herself."

"My deah, did you say the Stonecleft? How irritating!" Shirley murmured, once more assuming the grand manner of Marcia Lyman. "I really cawn't stay theah!"

"Maybe she will go back to Hollywood," suggested Rosalie.

"Then where would the picture be?" Anne asked.

"If you ask me, I think the picture would be better off," declared Lois. "If she is to take the part of a college student as the lead in the picture, it won't be any good. She hasn't any pep. I'll bet she wouldn't know how to hit a tennis ball."

"She doesn't take—peppy parts," explained Shirley. "She is the silent, sophisticated type."

"Then deliver me from them," begged Lenora. "I don't fancy her kind."

"Did you see the surprised look on Connie Elwood's face when she saw us being introduced to the star?" chortled Shirley.

"She was dumbfounded," said Lois gleefully.

"I wonder where the leading man is?" murmured Lenora. "Surely there is to be one in the picture!"

"I hope so," promptly declared Lois.

"Aha! So you have but one interest in this production?" Shirley said dramatically. "A man! Tsk, tsk! Have you no artistic sense? You should be interested merely for the sake of drama."

"I'll bet you would like to meet him," defended Lois.

"Well, I—ah—of course I would condescend to be introduced to him," Shirley conceded.

The others laughed.

"Who wouldn't?" murmured Rosalie.

"Let's have a game of tennis and forget the movies for a while," proposed Anne.

"As our star player, Beverly Gray, you have sadly been neglecting your duties at practice," Shirley said, frowning on her friend.

"There are a lot of things I've neglected," Beverly said readily enough. "I wonder if I'll ever catch up with things."

In her sophomore year at Vernon, Beverly and Anne had gone out for the tennis team. They had succeeded in making the second team, and the following year they climbed onto the first team. They had had matches with other girls' colleges, and always Vernon had made a brilliant showing. But this year they were rather weak. Beverly and Anne were the only seniors on the team, and they were _y far the best players. But despite their weakness they had succeeded in defeating the other colleges until they stood second in line for the championship. The championship was to be decided next week when they met Wayne Seminary on the home courts. The match was to be played for a silver loving cup, which would go into the possession of the winning team, proclaiming them champions of the Eastern Girls' Colleges.

"Connie Elwood and Kathleen Ryan have been out every day to practice," volunteered Anne. "I've seen them."

"I haven't really had a chance to do much practice," Beverly said ruefully. "Class and Hall duties keep me so occupied I scarcely have a minute to myself."

"It's a shame," burst out Rosalie. "Seniors should have a good time, but you spend all your time working."

"I like it," Beverly assured her.

"You should feel important," declared Lois. "Everybody turns to you for advice."

"Everybody but Connie Elwood," said Beverly dryly. "Every time I see her she has something to complain about."

"She would," Shirley said stormily. "She——"

"Are we to play tennis or not?" interrupted Anne.

"We are," Lenora said decisively, and led the way to the courts.

THE NEXT MORNING notices were posted on the bulletin boards in each dormitory house to the effect that there would be an honorary competition contest for a scenario to be filmed by the Forsythe Film Company. Any girl, whether freshman or senior, might write a scenario and submit it to the judges, who were Miss Wilder, the Dean, Mr. Forsythe, and two other members of the faculty. The winning story, if worthy, would be the one to be filmed on the campus. It would be quite a feather in the cap of the winner, and her classmates would most certainly fête her innumerable times. Only two weeks were allowed in which to write and submit a story, because that was all the time the film company could afford to wait.

Girls gathered about the bulletin board, and the air was filled with the buzz of excited conversation. Over the breakfast table the contest was discussed, and afterward the girls went back for another look at the notice to be sure they had made no mistake.

"There you are, Beverly," Lenora declared. "There is your chance to really write something."

"I wish I could," murmured Beverly.

"Surely you are going to enter the contest?" a laughing voice asked behind them.

Beverly turned smilingly to face Connie Elwood. "Are you?" she asked.

"I wouldn't miss the chance," Connie said confidently. "In fact, I think I'll win."

Lenora laughed loudly. "Not with all the Alphas entering a story."

"Too bad there isn't a money prize," Connie said sadly. "My allowance is pretty low."

"Isn't the honor enough?" Beverly asked humorously.

"Ye-e-es," Connie said slowly, "but——"

"It will be an honor if you win it," Lenora said.

"Why shouldn't I win?" Connie demanded. "After all, the Alphas aren't the only ones on the campus." She grinned. "Tell you what let's do, if one of the Alphas wins, my crowd will treat at Weller's."

"Fine!" applauded Lenora.

"But," Connie continued, "if one of us wins, you will have to treat our crowd."

"We'll agree," said Lenora and Beverly together.

"Meanwhile," Connie said smiling, "we have two weeks in which to compose a scenario."

"What happens if someone who isn't in either the Alphas or your crowd wins?" asked Lenora.

"Then neither of us gets a treat," answered Connie as she moved away.

"I don't like that possibility," grumbled Lenora.

Beverly laughed. "Why don't you ask Miss Marcia Lyman to treat you?"

"What? Take Miss Hollywood herself to Weller's?" Lenora frowned loftily on her friend. "She wouldn't condescend to walk down Main Street. Did you hear what she did the other day? She——"

"Ahoy, there, fellow Alphas!" Lois descended on them with a whirl.

Lenora gleefully imparted the news of the wager she and Beverly had made with Connie Elwood. Lois received the information enthusiastically. The three then routed out their other three members and together the six exchanged suggestions as to scenario plots. Each one was determined to submit a story. By some means they had to defeat their campus enemies—Connie and her friends. But when they tried to put their thoughts down on paper, the girls found that writing a scenario was a lot more difficult than just discussing it.

Lois gave up entirely and declared that she was

quite ready to pay her share of the treat which
was their wager. She wasn't and never would be a
writer, and Rosalie and Anne heartily agreed that
they felt the same way. When these three tore up
their attempts, it left only Lenora, Beverly, and
Shirley to uphold the honor of the Alphas, as
Lenora expressed it. Shirley, too, before the two
weeks were up, declared herself discouraged and
destroyed her manuscript. Lenora firmly insisted
that she would not give up, and she didn't. Day
after day, after classes were through, Lenora
labored over her story. She had no hope of winning, but she was determined to enter a story, at
least.

Beverly, too, between all her other activities,
found time to write. The tennis championship
match that was scheduled for the next week had
been postponed until the spring because several
girls on the Wayne team were ill, and their team
would be sadly incompetent without them. This
postponement left the time that Beverly should
have spent at practice open for her writing, and
she seized it joyfully. Hours she spent writing at
her portable typewriter, or staring into space,
groping in her mind for the phrase to best express
her thoughts. When she had finished it, she surveyed it triumphantly. It was rather good, she decided modestly. It was good, but not good enough

to win the contest. She would have to make some changes in the characters, they didn't exactly satisfy her. She spent more hours on it, correcting and adding to it.

Shirley, coming in early from a class, found Connie Elwood in the room, engrossed in Beverly's manuscript.

"What are you doing here?" Shirley demanded inhospitably.

"I came down to see Beverly," Connie answered frowning.

"When she wasn't in, I suppose you decided to read her story," Shirley said.

"You don't think I want to steal the idea——" Connie began.

"How do I know what you wanted to do?" Shirley said coldly. "You aren't exactly friends with Beverly, you know."

"But I wouldn't take her idea for a story," defended Connie. "It was lying here, and I just picked it up when you burst in. I haven't read it yet."

"Indeed?" Shirley murmured unconvinced.

"Besides," Connie continued, "I'm not entering a story in the contest."

"That's what you say," Shirley retorted.

Connie was noted for her impulsiveness and sudden gusts of temper, but on this occasion she restrained herself admirably.

"Shirley, what is the matter with you? Are you deliberately trying to quarrel with me?"

Shirley smiled loftily and opened the door. "Do you mind if I ask you to leave?"

"I won't leave until I find out what is wrong between you and me," Connie insisted. "I know there is no cause for friendship between us. Goodness knows, my crowd and the Alphas have been at odds for a long time. But the other girls in the Alpha Delta are at least friendly enemies."

Shirley remained silent, standing by the open door.

"Have I ever done anything to you?" Connie continued in mystification. "If so——"

"You've said some pretty mean things about Beverly and me and the rest of us," Shirley volunteered at last.

"I know I did last term," Connie admitted. "I still have my private opinion of what I think of you," she smiled, "but I never really harmed you."

Shirley merely smiled, and the baffling smile served to further infuriate Connie.

"I'd appreciate it if you would leave my room," Shirley said again.

"Maybe I'm stubborn, but I want to know why

you walk around with a chip continually on your shoulder," Connie insisted.

Shirley frowned. "I didn't invite you to knock it off," she said. "Listen, Connie, I won't bother you if you stay away from me. We won't ever be friends, because we don't think the same way. We are as different as the north and south poles. I don't see why you should worry in the first place," she said shortly. "Are you thinking of becoming friends with the Alpha Deltas?"

"Gracious, no," Connie said determinedly. "We would make fine sorority sisters, wouldn't we? I've no desire to declare war on anyone." She walked to the door. "When Beverly comes in, you might tell her I think her story is fine."

Shirley stared after the girl and then slammed the door violently. Of all the insolence! Calmly walking into their room and, of all things, reading Beverly's story. Doubtless she would immediately go out and write her own scenario, using Beverly's idea.

Beverly entered hurriedly, flinging her books to one side and grabbing up her story.

"Where are you going in such a rush?" Shirley asked.

"Going to hand my story to the contest judges," announced Beverly, "before I lose courage."

"But, Beverly——"

"Sorry, Shirley, can't stop now. I'll be back in a jiffy and we can talk then."

"But Connie was——"

"Ta-ta!"

The slamming of the door behind Beverly cut off Shirley's words. It would be no use to tell her about Connie when she returned, for her story would already be in the judges' hands. Shirley took her textbook and flung herself across the bed. It was seldom that she allowed herself to give way to such an overpowering dislike as she had for Connie Elwood. She detested the girl thoroughly. Things the girl had done to Beverly and to all of them rose uppermost in her mind. Connie had a nerve to ask her, Shirley, why she disliked her. She could have given Connie a hundred answers. She and her chums had done their best to thwart any plans the Alphas made this term.

Beverly came back a moment later, and they fell to discussing an assignment for the morrow.

"By the way," Beverly interrupted, "what was it you wanted to tell me?"

"Oh, nothing," Shirley said. "It doesn't matter in the least."

She hastily changed the subject lest Beverly should pry too deep, and there was really no reason now to tell her. It wouldn't do any good and might only worry her.

"Behold!" Lenora shouted, bursting in upon them. "A masterpiece!" She waved her manuscript over her head. "The scenario—she eez feeneshed!"

"Perfect imitation of the French professor," applauded Shirley.

"What do you call this—work of art?" asked Beverly.

"*A Senior's Dilemma, or They Shall Not Pass*," Lenora answered promptly. "I am on my way to the judges with it now. Come along?"

"I have to look over this lesson for tomorrow," Shirley declined.

"And I have to look over plans for a fiction dance some of the girls have submitted to me," Beverly contributed. "Would you girls be in favor of a fiction dance?" she asked.

"Sure," Lenora said. "What is it?"

Beverly explained. "Everyone is to go dressed as some famous person in fiction. We were thinking of giving it about Hallowe'en. Does that suit you girls?"

Shirley and Lenora nodded.

"Is it only a senior affair?" Lenora asked.

"We haven't decided yet," Beverly answered. "But if that is the wish of the majority, we will keep it strictly among the seniors."

"Well, I've got to be off." Lenora jumped up from where she had subsided beside Shirley on the bed. "The contest closes day after tomorrow, and I want to get this wonderful scenario in."

Two days later all the scenarios were in the hands of the judges, and there weren't many of them. More than one girl had started out in a fire of enthusiasm, but had given up in disappointment. A scenario was not as easy to write as some of them had believed.

Lenora was living in a fever of suspense. If she or Beverly couldn't win, she sincerely hoped that none of Connie Elwood's friends would walk off with the honors. The other Alphas shared her anxiety. It mattered vitally to them that their enemies should not triumph over them. They knew that defeat at the hands of Connie and her pals would not be easy. For one thing their popularity would be sadly depleted, but what mattered more than that was that Connie and the others would never get done talking about it. They would brag about their triumph as long as there was anyone to listen to them.

It took the judges three days to read the manuscripts submitted and to decide on the best one. Notices were posted to the effect that the winner would be announced in the auditorium after classes this afternoon. The girls were all excited. At last they would know whose story was considered worthy to be filmed.

"I'm all a-twitter," chirped Lenora as the six Alphas made their way to the auditorium after their last class.

"Remember that I like chocolate ice cream," Connie called across to them.

"We should remember?" shouted Lois. "You are the ones who are going to treat."

Connie and her chums laughed and continued on their way.

"I didn't like that laugh," declared Lenora frowning. "It had an ominous sound."

"Do you think they will keep their word about treating at Weller's?" Rosalie asked.

"Of course they will, and so shall we," Beverly said.

"We always pay our bets," added Lenora. "But we won't have to pay."

"I wish I had your optimism," Anne laughed.

"Personally, I don't think a girl from either our crowd or Connie's will win," declared Beverly.

"I'm inclined to agree with you," Shirley said.

"Don't say that," grieved Lenora. "Think of my *Senior's Dilemma.*"

"Well, we won't have to wait long," Rosalie comforted them. "My, isn't there a crowd in here!"

The auditorium was indeed crowded. It seemed as if all the girls on the campus desired to see whose scenario was to be filmed by the Forsythe Film Company. The girl who won would certainly be popular and envied. Nearly all the seats were taken, but the Alphas managed to find six together near the back. Their chief rivals were seated about four rows in front of them and flung impish grins back at the six Alphas.

Miss Wilder stood up and signaled for order. Instantly a hush fell over the expectant guests. At last the moment for the big news had arrived.

"All of the manuscripts submitted are good," she said after a few preliminary remarks, "but there are two that are outstanding. I have the honor to announce that the manuscript entitled *Stepping Stone,* by Miss Beverly Gray of the senior class, has won first place, while the comedy entitled *A Senior's Dilemma,* by Lenora Whitehill, also of the senior class, deserves honorable mention."

A silence held the audience for a moment after this announcement and then cries of "Gray! Beverly Gray! Whitehill! Lenora Whitehill!" rang through the auditorium. "Speech! Speech!" Lois and Shirley smilingly escorted the two contest winners to the stage. Beverly and Lenora blushingly and delightedly expressed their thanks, and a moment later were surrounded by a chattering, admiring bevy of girls. Both Alphas were completely overwhelmed by surprise. Neither one had expected to capture any honors at all, and now for them both to be winners——

"I can't quite believe it," declared Beverly, expressing the sentiments of all the Alphas.

"I'm afraid I'm dreaming," echoed Lenora. "Ow, what's the idea?" she demanded as Lois vigorously pinched her arm.

"I was merely demonstrating that you aren't dreaming," explained her friend.

"You don't have to be so hearty about it," grumbled Lenora. "Where is Connie Elwood?"

"Right here," that individual spoke up from behind Lenora. "Congratulations," she said dryly.

Lenora beamed on her. "I like vanilla ice cream, Connie," she declared.

Connie laughed good-naturedly. "Drop in at Weller's next Friday night," she invited.

"We'll be there," Lenora and Lois promised gleefully, and the other Alphas nodded assent.

The girls went on then to Chadwick Hall for dinner, Lenora and Beverly still surrounded by admiring lower classmen.

CHAPTER V

The Star

THE NEXT DAY, being Saturday, Lenora and Beverly went in to Vernon to do a little shopping. They took their own good time, looking in windows and strolling through shops, purchasing ribbons and other little knick-knacks. Finally, as was usually the case whenever they were in Vernon, they finished off the afternoon in Weller's. Lois and Anne were playing tennis, Shirley was reading a book, and Rosalie was visiting another senior at Courtney Hall, so Beverly and Lenora were the only two Alphas in the ice-cream saloon. They lingered not very long over their refreshments, and as they made their way out onto the pavement two breathless sophomores ran up to them.

"Oh, Miss Gray, Miss Whitehill, will you play tennis with us on Wednesday?" the two gasped.

Beverly and Lenora conceded graciously, and the sophomores were more than thrilled.

"Ah, my public," Lenora sighed.

Beverly laughed. "Poor kids, they have terrible crushes."

"What do you mean 'poor kids'?" Lenora demanded indignantly. "When one has a crush one is in seventh heaven. They are to be envied. I remember, when I was a freshman, I had the most terrible crush on a senior. Oh, I thought everything she did was the personification of grace, goodness, and all the heavenly virtues. I got over it, though, when she completely ignored me. She didn't even know I was in the same world with her, so I finally became conscious that worshiping an idol from afar isn't at all satisfying and came down to earth with a bang."

"It wasn't very nice of her to completely ignore you," Beverly smiled.

"It was rather disappointing at times," Lenora admitted indifferently. "Several times I was heartbroken over the injustice of fate, as I called it then. Then she graduated, and I discovered that she really wasn't so great after all."

"A fallen star," Beverly laughed.

Lenora giggled. "Something like it. I say, isn't that Mr. Forsythe, of the Forsythe Film Company, and Miss Wilder there across the street from us?"

"Correct the first time," Beverly answered,

The girls crossed and exchanged greetings with the Dean and the moving-picture magnate.

"When are you going to start filming the picture, Mr. Forsythe?" Lenora asked.

"I'm afraid the picture is off indefinitely," Miss Wilder said slowly.

"Off?" Beverly and Lenora gasped.

"You mean you aren't going to make it?" Lenora demanded.

Mr. Forsythe nodded gloomily.

"But why?" Beverly asked.

"Miss Marcia Lyman left this morning for Hollywood," Miss Wilder explained.

"But what is she going to Hollywood for?" Lenora wanted to know. "Has she left the company flat?"

Mr. Forsythe smiled at the expression "flat" and nodded. "Yes, she has left. Cordial Pictures Company has offered her a new contract with a much higher salary, and she has taken it."

"But can't you get another star?" Beverly asked. "Surely there are more girls to be had."

"Most of our stars are tied up in other productions," Mr. Forsythe answered. "I guess there is nothing to do but to load our stuff back into our car and go to Hollywood."

If the picture company withdrew, the college would lose the sum of money it had been going to use to build an indoor swimming pool. This thought was in both girls' minds. Then Lenora had a brilliant idea.

"Mr. Forsythe," she said smiling broadly, "if you could star a girl who is a student at Vernon now, wouldn't it make the picture even more interesting? It would positively be a college picture then. Everybody in it, except the leading man, of course, would be students at Vernon. Would you do that?"

Mr. Forsythe smiled. "But where are we going to get a girl who can act?"

"We've got the very girl," Lenora declared. "She is a marvelous actress."

"Who is it, Lenora?" Miss Wilder asked.

"Shirley Parker," Beverly answered, and Lenora nodded.

"She could do it, couldn't she, Miss Wilder?" Lenora asked.

"I believe she could," the Dean said slowly.

"Well, where is this girl?" Mr. Forsythe asked impatiently. "Why haven't I seen her before? She might be material for a new star."

"We'll find her and bring her to you," Lenora and Beverly promised.

"Bring her to my private car for a screen test," Mr. Forsythe said. "If she is good and can act, we might use her. Remember, I only said might!"

"She'll be the biggest star you've ever had," Lenora assured him excitedly.

"We'll see, we'll see," the man answered as the two girls scampered off.

Lenora and Beverly dashed madly across the campus and into Chadwick Hall.

"Where is Shirley?" Lenora demanded of Rosalie, who was just coming down the steps.

"I don't know," that young lady answered.

"She must be upstairs," put in Beverly.

The two continued on their wild flight and burst in upon Shirley, the latter engaged in writing letters.

"What's the matter with you two?" she asked in surprise.

Lenora grabbed her by the hand. "Come along," she said urgently.

"B-but——" Shirley began protestingly.

"Don't argue," Lenora said breathlessly and pulled Shirley along to the door.

Shirley braced herself. "I won't go another step until you tell me what this is all about!"

"Here we are trying to make you a movie star and you won't even come along with us," wailed Lenora.

"What does she mean, Beverly?" Shirley demanded.

"Marcia Lyman left the movie company flat this morning and went back to Hollywood. The picture is all off unless Mr. Forsythe can find a girl to take her place," Beverly explained.

"But what has that to do with me?" Shirley asked wonderingly.

"Don't you see?" Lenora said, dancing in her impatience. "You are the girl. It is up to you to star in the picture. If the company leaves Vernon, we won't get that indoor swimming pool."

"But I've never been in the movies," Shirley protested. "I don't know the first thing about it."

"You've acted in plays," Lenora pointed out.

"Yes, but——"

"Mr. Forsythe said we should bring you over for a screen test," said Beverly.

"But I don't want to——"

"Jumping jellybeans!" Lenora shouted. "You want to be an actress, don't you? Here is your chance on a silver platter and you are scared to take it!"

"Of course I'm scared to take it," Shirley said firmly. "What if——"

"Don't be a Calamity Jane," Lenora urged. "Come along and take the screen test. If that isn't any good, you won't have to worry about acting in the picture."

"What do you think of it, Beverly?" Shirley appealed to her roommate.

"I'd take the test," Beverly said calmly.

"Anybody would," Lenora declared.

"All right," Shirley agreed suddenly. "Where do I take the test?"

"Fine!" Lenora said excitedly. "Come along."

Shirley, escorted triumphantly by Lenora and Beverly, went to Mr. Forsythe's improvised office in the private railway coach. She took the screen test, and while they and Mr. Forsythe watched the film being run off, they waited anxiously for his verdict.

"My dear girl, let me congratulate you," he said finally after the film had ended. "You have the makings of a great star. You shall play the lead in this film, and we will draw up a contract for you to come to Hollywood."

Shirley received this announcement in amazed silence. A career had been dumped in her lap and she scarcely recognized it. The other two Alphas were equally amazed and delighted. They rushed Shirley back to Chadwick Hall to spread the good news around. Anne and Rosalie and Lois were speechless with surprise. At first they thought the three were playing a joke on them, but it finally became clear that Shirley and Beverly and Lenora were in dead earnest.

Two days later Shirley started working in the film. She had a young, handsome, talented man playing opposite her, and the girls felt a tinge of envy at her good fortune. The story of the picture was the story of a young writer, played by the leading man, Conway Grant, who came to the little college town looking for material for his next novel. He met a college senior, played by Shirley, and various complications arose from their acquaintance. It was an interesting, adventurous plot, and the characters were vivid and alive. Other Vernon girls had small parts, and among them was Lois, who was to play the part of Shirley's chum in the picture.

It did not take the Alpha girls long to notice that this rush of success was becoming a little too much for Shirley. She was beginning to seem aloof from them. She no longer took the interest in college affairs that she, as a senior, should have. All her time was devoted to the picture—and to Conway Grant. Only two weeks had passed, but it might well have been two years, so far had Shirley grown away from her friends. Of course, she deigned to recognize them and occasionally stopped to chat, but it was not the same Shirley as of a year ago. She was conscious, now, of her importance, and moved as if in a different world. Many times the girls met her and Conway Grant strolling down

Main Street and received merely a casual nod, as if they were nothing but the merest acquaintances. At such times Lenora and Lois would exchange significant glances that would eventually bode no good for Shirley.

CHAPTER VI

A Proposal

BEVERLY was in her room reading a lesson for the morrow when Shirley came in. Dinner had been over long ago, and study hour was half through. Shirley had been absent from the dinner table, and now Beverly looked for an explanation.

"Hello," she said pleasantly. "Been working again?"

"Where else?" Shirley asked. She took a beret and a scarf from the closet and turned again to the door.

"Where are you going?" Beverly wanted to know. Her eyes had shadowed at the coldness of Shirley's brusque answer to her former question.

"Mr. Grant is taking me to the movies," Shirley answered. "Does it matter to you?"

"Yes," Beverly said, "it does. Have you asked permission from Mrs. Dennis?"

"Of course not," Shirley said loftily. "I don't have to."

"You may think you don't," Beverly said calmly. "But remember, Shirley, you are a studen⊦ at Vernon, regardless of your work in the movin₍ picture."

"I'm the star in the picture," Shirley said grandly.

"You still have to ask permission to go into town after study hour," Beverly insisted.

"Are you trying to quarrel with me?" Shirley demanded, frowning.

"Of course not," Beverly said promptly. "We haven't quarreled for almost three years, why should we start now? I'm merely telling you something. I'm in charge of the girls here, and I won't have my roommate disobeying rules that I expect the other girls to keep."

"Are you forbidding me to go out?" Shirley asked belligerently.

Beverly laid her book aside resignedly and stood up. "You're a senior, Shirley, you know what is right and what is wrong. If you go out without permission, it is my duty to report you to Mrs. Dennis."

"Duty!" Shirley scoffed. "You think a lot of that word, don't you?"

Beverly's lips tightened, but she checked her

temper. "You used to, too. It is a word none of us can afford to forget. Are you going to Mrs. Dennis?" she asked after a moment.

"I suppose I must," Shirley said darkly, and went out, slamming the door behind her.

Beverly stared at the closed door reflectively for a moment and then turned to the window. She knelt on a cushion and let the early October breeze ruffle her curls. The moon came out from behind a cloud, and its silver light flooded the campus, throwing the buildings into dark relief against the sky. Stars twinkled like tiny lanterns overhead. Beverly rested her chin on her folded arms, and her eyes were wistful.

Things between herself and Shirley were coming to a breach. Ever since work on the moving picture had begun Shirley was—different. The Alphas had at first thought she would get over it, but she did not. Every day had seen Shirley growing farther and farther away from her friends. Whether she considered herself above them they couldn't decide, but she acted as though she did. At the beginning of the term Shirley had been jolly and fun-loving, a perfect roommate. But now she was reserved, aloof, almost cross. Beverly had at first attributed Shirley's strained attitude to the fact that the picture work was new and strenuous, but now she knew better. Even difficult work could not account for Shirley's sarcastic and touchy attitude toward the Alphas. Lately, the girls had started avoiding Shirley, and Beverly could not find it in her heart to blame them. Their senior year should have been full to the brim of good times and pleasant companionship. They all wanted something pleasant by which to remember their last school days. Shirley was missing all that should have made her senior term memorable.

Funny, how success went to one's head. Shirley considered herself a big success now, but her classmates considered her small. A girl who could so completely change didn't deserve success. She had no mental balance, no—character. Beverly thought of a saying she had once heard—"Be nice to the people you meet on the road up, for they are the same ones you meet on the road down." When Shirley's star fell, as stars inevitably do, would she be able to regain her old place with her friends? The ones like Shirley who had success thrown at them and didn't know the meaning of working and striving for that success inevitably grew conceited with their own importance. They felt sufficient unto themselves. Yet, when their success crumpled in their grasp, what did they have? Nothing.

Beverly vowed then and there that if ever she achieved success in her chosen field as a writer, she would not let it interfere with her friendships. If ever she acquired the position which she hoped some day to have, she would remember those she knew and loved always. She would not let herself become conceited with her own importance. If she ever did, if she ever thought herself as above her friends, she hoped that——

A loud knocking at the door brought her down to earth. She stood up and faced about.

"Come in," she called.

"Miss Gray." A freshman stood on the threshold, and she was sadly disheveled and nervous.

"Heavens, what happened to you?" Beverly asked in surprise.

"Some girls have been playing pranks, and I don't think it is a bit funny," the freshman said a trifle hysterically. "They—they——"

"Who were they?" Beverly asked.

"I don't know exactly," the freshman answered. "But I'm going to report this outrage to Mrs. Dennis."

"I wouldn't do that," Beverly said kindly. "After all, a freshman must expect some pranks. Be a good sport about it and go back to your room and go to bed," Beverly advised smiling. "I'll try to prevent anything of the kind from happening in the future."

"Do you mean to say you aren't going to do anything about it?" the freshman demanded.

"What can I do?" Beverly asked. "You don't know who they were."

"I think it was Connie Elwood and her crowd," the freshman answered. "When I passed her room just now I heard a lot of talking and laughing."

Beverly looked a bit dubious. What could she do?

"If you don't do something immediately, I am going to report it to Mrs. Dennis," the freshman insisted.

"But——" Beverly began.

"I *am* going to Mrs. Dennis," the girl cried and whirled from the room.

Beverly sank into a chair, a frown on her face. This job of being in charge of the girls was becoming irksome. She had no full authority, just enough to make it difficult. She had rather thought her troubles with Connie and her crowd were through when the Alphas, minus Shirley, had dined with them at Weller's last Friday night, payment of the bet over the scenario contest. But now it seemed Connie and the others were up to their old tricks again. Beverly sighed and opened her book. Let the freshman report to Mrs. Dennis, and let Mrs. Dennis take care of the matter herself. Beverly was tired and she didn't propose to enter a quarrel just because some freshman couldn't stand a few jokes being played on her.

Another knock on the door interrupted her reading, and she called an impatient "Come."

Lenora poked her head in. "Hi, Snookums! Reading?"

"Trying to," Beverly smiled. "Come in and make yourself comfy. I've been having my troubles with a freshman."

Lenora listened sympathetically while Beverly poured out the story of Connie and her friends' latest doings. They started talking then about the fiction dance to be given on Hallowe'en, until Beverly interrupted.

"By the way, what brings you here?" she asked. "I thought you had a big assignment to study."

"I have," Lenora said seriously. "But I can't study."

"Why not?" Beverly asked.

"To tell the truth," Lenora began, "I came to complain, too. You know Connie's room is directly above mine, and they are making such an uproarious racket that it is impossible to think. I went up and threatened to have the whole bunch up before Miss Wilder tomorrow, but it didn't do any good."

"What's going on in there tonight?" Beverly murmured irritably. "I suppose I shall have to go up."

Another knock on the door, and Beverly pulled it open. Two sophomores, with dark frowns on their faces, stood there.

"Miss Gray," began one of the sophomores, "we've come to complain about——"

"Don't tell me," Beverly interrupted. "I know—Connie Elwood."

"Yes. We have an important examination tomorrow," the one girl continued, "but because our room is next to hers we can't study for the noise."

"We are going to Mrs. Dennis," the other sophomore added, "if it isn't stopped."

Beverly felt like telling them to go ahead and report it to Mrs. Dennis if it would make them happy, but she didn't. Instead, she assured them she would do all she could to restore peace and quiet to Chadwick Hall. The sophomores returned to their room slightly mollified, and Beverly grinned at Lenora.

"Now to beard the lion in her den," she said opening the door again.

"Want me to come along—as reinforcement?" Lenora asked.

Beverly shook her head. "I'll manage," she said.

She made her way to the fifth floor and paused at the top of the steps. Hilarious sounds were coming from behind Connie Elwood's door, and Beverly wondered that they had not been audible even

down in her room. Connie and her friends were
certainly having a rousing good time tonight. If
Mrs. Dennis should come up here and note the
noise and merriment, Connie and her friends
would have a sad surprise. There would be punish-
ment for the lot of them, for Mrs. Dennis could
be stern when she wished. Such joyousness was not
allowed to disturb the other pupils.

Beverly knocked on Connie's door, and instantly
all sound in the room died away. She turned the
knob and swung open the door. Connie and her
friends were caught in mad attempts at flight. If
the situation had not been deadly serious, she would
have laughed outright at the expressions of panic
on their faces.

"What's going on here?" she demanded in the
sternest tone of voice she possessed.

"A picnic," Connie rejoined flippantly.

"Rather a noisy one, don't you think?" asked
Beverly. "Even though you are on the fifth floor
and far enough away from Mrs. Dennis' office, you
are not allowed to raise the roof."

"I suppose that freshman told on us," burst out
Evelyn DeLong.

Beverly smiled. "No one needed to tell on you.
You are making yourself heard all over the building. I think you better adjourn this meeting until
tomorrow."

"We'll do no such thing," Connie declared. "This is my room, my friends can come here any time they like."

"Of course they can," Beverly said agreeably, "but I'm telling them to leave now before they get into trouble."

"What trouble?" Virginia Harris demanded.

"Mrs. Dennis is on her way up here," Beverly said idly.

"I don't believe it," Connie denied. "If she is on her way up here, why did you come? You are trying to scare us."

Beverly smiled. "I'm not trying to scare you. You had better go to your rooms now, girls," she said to the others.

After a minute of moody silence in which the girls stared back and forth defiantly, the party began to break up. Ada Collins and Virginia Harris drifted off to their room farther down the hall. Phyllis Tanner and Evelyn DeLong went into their room across the hall, and Connie Elwood and Kathleen Ryan rebelliously cleared up the wreckage in their room. Beverly waited until the last vestige of the party had disappeared, and then she went out, closing the door behind her.

She had no sooner closed the door than Mrs. Dennis' voice hailed her. "Miss Gray, where is the

—party that the girls have been complaining about?"

"It is over," Beverly answered.

"Such a thing is not allowed in Chadwick Hall," Mrs. Dennis continued sternly. "Tell me who the girls are and I will see them in the morning."

"I don't know who they are," Beverly answered smiling.

Mrs. Dennis regarded Beverly closely for a moment, and then her frown cleared and she too smiled. It was quite evident that Beverly knew who the girls were but didn't want to tell.

"Very well, Miss Gray, but the next time you hear of such a disturbance, I wish you would come to me."

"I will, Mrs. Dennis," Beverly promised, and without a backward glance she turned to follow the house mistress down the steps.

Shirley had not yet returned when Beverly got back to her room. Beverly had been tempted to ask Mrs. Dennis if she had given Shirley permission to leave Chadwick Hall, but thought better of it. She had no intention of spying on her roommate. If Shirley broke the rule and was caught she had only herself to blame. Beverly undressed in darkness and crawled into bed. For a long time she lay awake, staring up at the ceiling, thinking.

She thought about her home back in Renville

and of the Lucky Circle, as the group of her friends had styled themselves. One of the Lucky Circle, Jim Stanton, the boy who had been Beverly's chum ever since little-girl days, was out in Wyoming on an engineering job. It was a year now that he had been gone, and in all that time she had not seen him. Of course they had written to one another regularly, but letters at best are unsatisfactory things. She wondered how he was, if he liked his work. He scarcely wrote about the job itself, filling his letters with news of little, unexpected incidents that were at times humorous and pathetic. She wondered when the work would be finished and he could come back East again. She hoped that he could come home for Christmas.

In the morning Shirley greeted Beverly very briefly and withdrew into herself. Beverly, hurt and disappointed more and more each day by her friend's attitude, summoned her pride and struggled to appear as unconcerned as ever. If Shirley wanted to terminate their old friendship, she would not cry over it.

The day was full of events for her, and when she finally made her way back to the Hall for a few moments' rest before dinner she was tired. Classes had been difficult, she had played three games of basketball, had discussed and planned events for the forthcoming fiction dance, had listened to an endless tale of complaints about different things in the Hall, and now she was discouraged. Her spirits lagged, and for a while she considered resigning from the position of president of the class and also the charge of the girls in the Hall. But she rebuked herself. It was a high honor to be president of her class, and she would do the best she could. Things only seemed difficult because she was tired. She threw herself across the bed, and in a moment she was asleep.

It was thus that Connie Elwood found her. Connie had come humbly, it was true, to thank Beverly for being such a sport last night and not telling Mrs. Dennis who had had the party. She and her friends had had a long talk this afternoon, and they agreed that they might have been wrong in their estimation of Beverly. If Beverly hated them, as they supposed she did, she would not have lost such an opportunity as last night afforded her to get even for some of the things they had done to her. Connie had come to Beverly's room this afternoon, figuratively speaking, with the olive branch of peace. She and her friends were willing to put an end to their warlike opposition to Beverly and to forget the past.

Receiving no answer to her knock on the door, Connie had turned the knob and walked in. When she first saw Beverly lying on the bed, she had thought the girl might be sick, but she had easily determined that Beverly was merely asleep. She stood staring down at the slender figure on the bed, and a frown appeared between her brows. Beverly looked tired; she had been working too hard with class affairs. Connie felt a tinge of shame when she thought that she and her friends were responsible for some of that tiredness of Beverly's. She drew a silken coverlet over Beverly and looked up at the door suddenly, flushing guiltily.

Lenora stood on the threshold taking in the scene with astonished eyes. Slowly the mingled surprise and displeasure that always appeared on her face when she saw Connie Elwood faded, and a smile twisted the corners of her lips. She motioned Connie from the room and closed the door. When the two girls stood face to face, Lenora held out her hand.

"Is the war over, Connie?"

"It's over," Connie said, grasping Lenora's extended hand in a firm grip. "We want to be friends with the Alpha Deltas."

"Why this sudden decision, if I might ask?" Lenora laughed.

"Beverly did it," Connie said truthfully.

"She does most things around here," Lenora declared.

"She is tired," Connie said, frowning. "She has

been working too hard with the class and the Hall."

"Let's take the Hall difficulties off her shoulders," Lenora proposed. "With your friends and the Alphas working together we can keep things peaceful around here."

"We'll do our part," Connie promised.

"And now," Lenora proposed smilingly, slipping an arm into Connie's, "let's go to Weller's to celebrate our new—peace treaty."

CHAPTER VII

A Quarrel

Two days later the Alphas were gathered in Beverly's and Shirley's room talking when Beverly entered. Shirley was working on a scene from the picture, and none of the girls knew when she could get away.

"I called this special meeting of the Alpha Deltas to propose something," Lenora began.

"It better be good," warned Lois. "You pulled me away from basketball practice."

"I'm sure you will be interested," murmured Lenora.

"What is it?" Rosalie asked.

"It must be important," declared Beverly, "for the last twenty-four hours Lenora has been going around with a cat-who-swallowed-the-canary expression on her face."

"Are you accusing me of deceit?" mourned Lenora. "You know everything I do has the thought of good for the Alphas at its base."

"Come on, out with it," Lois demanded. "When you start paying compliments you want something."

"Have you noticed," Lenora continued, without a glance at Lois, "how Connie Elwood and her chums have improved in behavior?"

"Very slightly," drawled Lois.

"They have conducted themselves rather nicely these past two days," Beverly said thoughtfully. "I noticed it, but I can't account for it."

"It won't last," Lois declared.

"Evelyn and Kathleen invited me into Weller's yesterday," Rosalie volunteered, "and I nearly fainted, the invitation was so unexpected."

"I hope you rallied?" Lois murmured.

"Indeed I did," Rosalie declared. "I never let an opportunity like that slip past."

"We might have known," said Lenora. "But to get back to business, have any of the rest of you noticed an improvement in our erstwhile enemies?"

"Ada and Phyllis walked back from Chapel with me yesterday," Anne said, "and they were most friendly. I can't understand it."

"It won't last," Lois said again. "Those girls never behaved themselves for more than two days before. If they continue along this line they will explode."

"I can explain it," Lenora said smiling broadly.

"What is it?" Lois asked.

"They want to join the Alpha Delta Sorority," Lenora announced, gleefully noting the effect of this announcement on the others.

Lois nearly fell off her chair. "They want to what?" she shouted.

"They have buried the hatchet and want to be friends," Lenora continued. "Is that so strange?"

"I'll say it's strange," murmured Anne.

"It's unbelievable," Lois declared. "Do my ear deceive me or did I hear aright? Please say that again."

Patiently Lenora repeated it. "They want to join up with the Alphas."

"Oh, this is too much," Lois said dramatically. "Whatever moved them to such a momentous decision?"

"Never mind," Lenora evaded. "The point is, they want to join. What do you say?"

"It would be nice to take in some new members," Beverly said.

"If they don't start to quarrel the minute they join with us," Anne said.

"How do you know they want to join?" Rosalie asked her roommate.

"Connie told me," Lenora answered. "Let's take them in."

"I'm in favor of it," Beverly agreed.

"All right," Anne nodded.

"I'll agree," said Rosalie.

"Are you sure they want to join?" Lois asked again. "I can't believe it."

"Of course I'm sure," Lenora said impatiently. "Are you agreeable, Lois?"

"I'll try anything once," Lois said resignedly.

"Then we are all agreed that——" Lenora was beginning when Shirley walked in.

Shirley looked about the circle and nodded a cool greeting. The girls exchanged glances.

"Shirley," Beverly began, "Lenora has just proposed that——"

"We let Connie and her friends join the Alpha Deltas," finished Lenora.

"You can let them join," Shirley said unconcernedly, "but if they do, I shall resign."

"Shirley!" Beverly said in surprise.

"What's the matter?" Anne seconded.

"Don't you like Connie?" Rosalie asked.

"No, I don't," Shirley admitted readily with a frown.

"You like very few people these days, don't you?" Lois murmured slowly.

"What do you mean?" Shirley swung on her.

Not for nothing had Lois been nicknamed Truth, and now she spoke out straight from the shoulder.

"You've gone high-hat on us, haven't you?"

Shirley colored. "I don't see that it concerns you what I do."

"Wait until a wind storm comes along and blows that high hat off, you won't——"

"I won't ask you to pick it up," Shirley interrupted. "I know each one of you is jealous of my chance in the movies."

"Jealous!" Lois laughed. "That's a good joke."

"It's true, and you know it," Shirley said angrily. "Each one of you has hated to see me become the star in the picture."

"The trouble with you is you have a crush on that leading man, Conway Grant," Lenora burst out.

"He has nothing to do with it," Shirley flamed. "Haven't I a right to talk to whom I please? Must I answer to you for my actions?"

"Of course not," Lois soothed. "But we didn't like to see you becoming so conceited over——"

"Conceited, am I?" Shirley demanded wrathfully. "If you think so, I don't see why you bother to talk to me. In fact, I would prefer that you didn't."

"You needn't worry, I shan't any more," Lois said firmly.

With a final scathing glance about at the girls, Shirley departed.

"I don't see why she should feel so big," Anne said indignantly.

"Beverly wrote the scenario, and that was just as important as Shirley's part, yet Beverly isn't conceited. Where are you going?" Lois demanded.

Beverly had risen and run to the door. Without answering Lois she ran down the hall after Shirley. Shirley was descending the stairs, and Beverly followed her. She caught up with Shirley in the living room.

"Shirley, don't be angry. The girls didn't mean the things they said."

"Well, I meant what I said," Shirley declared. "None of you need ever speak to me again."

"Don't be foolish," Beverly said, half smiling. "This is our senior year, we all want to be friends."

"Then go back to your—friends and let me alone," Shirley said coldly.

"But you are my roommate," Beverly pleaded, "I don't want——"

"Don't concern yourself about me," Shirley begged. "I'll see if I can have my room changed," she finished, pulling away.

Beverly stared after Shirley in utter astonishment. That last statement had amounted to as much as a slap in the face. Roommates separating in their last year—it was almost a tragedy. After four years, after weathering their first term of quarrels and disturbances, they had gone through happy months together to finish as total strangers. She felt a kindly hand on her shoulder and turned to face Connie Elwood.

"I couldn't help overhearing," Connie said gently. "I don't think she really means that."

Beverly summoned her pride and managed an indifferent shrug that did not totally conceal her feelings from the brown-eyed Connie.

"I'm rather inclined to think she does mean it," Beverly said slowly. "I've seen this coming on for weeks."

"She'll come back and apologize," Connie assured her, a friendly arm within Beverly's as the two mounted the stairs.

Beverly smiled ruefully. "You don't know Shirley. Her pride wouldn't let her. She is about finished with all the Alphas."

"That reminds me," Connie began, "has Lenora told you that we——"

"Want to join with us?" Beverly asked. "Yes, and as far as I'm concerned you are a member right now."

"Thanks, Beverly, we've treated you pretty meanly, and we're—sorry," Connie said earnestly. "And we don't want you to think——"

Beverly patted her hand gently. "We'll be friends from now on, shall we?"

"There is nothing I want more," Connie declared, and such a declaration coming from the rebellious Connie Elwood was a surprise.

CHAPTER VIII

Defeat

A WEEK passed, and during that week Shirley kept stubbornly to herself. She refused to meet with the Alphas and even to acknowledge them when they met by chance on the campus or on Main Street. She devoted herself to her work in the picture with almost an obsession. When she was not working she could usually be found talking or walking with her leading man. All this the girls viewed with growing disfavor. Girls with whom Shirley had once been friends began to avoid her. No longer was she one of the merry group that descended on Weller's many times during the week. She was not sought out to take part in any sports, and she did not offer her help in any college event.

Among the sports events of the term were the basketball games played between the four classes. Shirley, for the past two years, had been a shining light on the basketball team. Many of the old players had graduated last term, and now the senior basketball team was sadly in need of all of its regular members. Beverly and Lois were excellent players, but without Shirley, their support was poor. Other classmen were elected to the team, but none of them could replace the whirlwind Shirley.

In turn, the seniors met each class team, and somehow they managed to triumph over the freshmen and sophomores. The junior class, too, had triumphed over the lower classmen, and now it was up to the seniors and juniors to meet and decide the championship of the school.

The juniors were good. They had a strong and fast team. Their members were light and fast, and they had practised hard. The seniors, too, had devoted much of their time to practice, but still they knew their team was weak. They needed Shirley to help them triumph over the juniors. Shirley could make more goals than any of the other girls, and the seniors needed her, or they would lose the most important game of the season.

"I'm willing to ask her to come out," Beverly said as she and Lois and Lenora walked back to Chadwick Hall after basketball practice.

"Why should you?" Lenora murmured. "You aren't captain of the team. Besides, I don't think she would come."

"We ought to explain to her just how much we

do need her playing this coming Friday night," Lois said thoughtfully. "Maybe she would come out just for this game."

"She hasn't been to practice since they started making that movie," Lenora continued reproachfully. "She couldn't waste her time playing in a mere basketball game."

"She should be willing to back her class," Beverly pointed out. "She is still a senior, and as such she should want to see us win."

"She might want us to win," Lois agreed. "But would she consent to help us win?"

"I doubt it," Lenora said flatly. "I wouldn't even ask her."

"I'm going to," Beverly said determinedly. "She might surprise us and agree to play."

"That would be a surprise," Lenora declared.

"I'll come with you," Lois offered to Beverly. "Perhaps two of us can persuade her."

"That's good," Beverly said, smiling ruefully. "I shall probably need a lot of help."

"Don't count on me," Lenora said bluntly. "I won't ask her."

"We didn't ask you to," Lois said firmly. "We'll do our best, and then if she doesn't play—we shall lose, that is all."

"Don't be pessimistic," Lenora urged. "A miracle might happen, and we might win."

"It would have to be a miracle," declared Lois. "You know perfectly well without Shirley we don't stand a chance."

"Well, if she is in our room now," Beverly said, "I shall ask her."

"I'll come up with you," Lois said again. "She will probably explode when she sees me, for she hasn't spoken to me since the other day when we asked her if she objected to Connie and the others joining the Alphas. I hope she doesn't bite me," she finished humorously.

"I shall wait here for the verdict," Lenora said lazily, sinking into a chair as they entered the living room. "If she should throw you down the steps, I'll catch you."

"Huh!" Lois murmured disgustedly. "I'd like to see her throw me down the steps."

Beverly and Lenora entered the former's room. Shirley was there, reading over the script to the picture. She didn't look up when the two entered, and Beverly and Lois exchanged glances. It was going to be more difficult than they had expected. Beverly laid her books on her desk and turned to face Shirley, while Lois looked uncomfortably about the room. The very set of Shirley's shoulders was forbidding, and she kept her gaze strictly on the pages before her.

"Shirley——" Beverly began uncertainly.

The red-headed girl looked up. "Well?"

"We'd like to talk to you," Beverly said, more uncomfortably this time.

"Go ahead," Shirley said calmly but not encouragingly.

"Why haven't you come out for basketball practice lately?" Lois asked.

"Because I haven't time," Shirley answered. "Besides, I'm not interested in basketball any more."

"We need you on the team to help beat the juniors next Friday night," Beverly continued. "Won't you come out for practice so you can play then?"

"No."

"But if you don't, we will lose the game," said Lois. "You should support your class."

"I haven't time to practise," Shirley said with finality and turned back to her script.

"But you could easily spare an hour a day for this week," Beverly pleaded. "The seniors have to win the game Friday night to be champions of the school."

"What do you want me to do about it?" Shirley asked unenthusiastically.

"Come out and play with us," Lois supplied. "You can do it easily—when our team needs you so badly."

Shirley shook her head. "I'm not going out for basketball any more," she said stiffly.

"Come on, Beverly," Lois said impatiently, "we are wasting our time. She is so taken up with herself she wouldn't do a thing for her class."

Shirley slammed down her script. "Listen, Lois, I didn't ask you to come up here. You know I don't have time to practise basketball, and that is all there is to it."

"I know," Lois said dryly. "You don't think it was easy for me to come up here, do you? I've got some pride, too. After the other day I vowed I wouldn't talk to you again, but now the team needs you, and I was willing to come halfway. But now you—you——"

"Lois, please," interrupted Beverly.

"You can take your old basketball team and jump in the lake with it," Shirley said angrily.

Lois left the room immediately, and Beverly confronted Shirley with a half smile.

"It wasn't necessary to be so—explosive," she said humorously.

"I meant what I said," Shirley said loftily. "She needn't think she can tell me what I should do. I——"

"She wasn't trying to," Beverly said. "She was just telling you that you had no right to fail your friends when we need you to win that game."

"They aren't my friends," Shirley said shortly.

"They were once upon a time," Beverly pointed out. "Won't you come out and play with us on Friday night?"

"No!" Shirley said angrily. "I don't care whether our class wins or not."

"And I'm sure none of the girls care whether you are a success in this movie or not," Beverly said candidly.

Shirley looked at her roommate in surprise as Beverly marched out and slammed the door. This was something else to think about. Was it possible that the girls really weren't interested in her movie career?

She rose and walked to the window, a worried frown on her face. Had Lois and Beverly been right in their attitude? Did she owe it to her classmates to play in the game Friday night? Perhaps she did, but she couldn't find the time to devote to practice. Another thought intruded itself in her mind. Beverly really was as busy as she was, yet Beverly found time to practise regularly. Of course Beverly's activities weren't as strenuous as hers, she assured herself. Just the same—— Should she play in that game Friday night? She had emphatically declared that she wouldn't, but she knew if she changed her mind the girls would let her.

She argued with herself for over an hour, but her doubts were quelled when Mr. Forsythe told her on Friday night they were going to take some of the night scenes for the picture. Now she had a good excuse, and it was impossible for her to play. But the girls hadn't given up yet. Beverly and Caroline Johnson, captain of the basketball team, met her on the campus the next afternoon.

"We've talked to Mr. Forsythe," Beverly began, "and he says he is willing to postpone the night scenes until next week if you are willing to play in the basketball game."

"No," Shirley answered.

"You mean you positively refuse?" Caroline asked.

"I mean that it wouldn't be fair to the other actors or to Mr. Forsythe," Shirley said. "He has spent a lot of money on this picture, and he wants to finish it as soon as possible. He and the others are all prepared to take the scenes on Friday night, and I don't want to postpone it."

The girls said no more but left her then. Shirley felt uncomfortable. She knew what she had said was said as much to comfort her own conscience as to convince the other girls. She knew the girls needed a good fast player on Friday night, and yet she was determined not to play, but to go on with the picture. After all, acting was her chosen career, and it meant more to her than a basketball game.

On Friday night the junior and senior teams gathered in the gymnasium. There was a crowd of spectators made up of lower and upper classmen alike. It was easily noticeable that the senior team was not in its best form. At previous games when Shirley had been whirling about the floor the other girls had had to exert themselves to keep up with her speedy pace. But tonight the girls lagged alarmingly. Beverly as center and Lois as forward did the best they could to keep the girls on their toes, but the juniors were steadily piling up a score against them. The ball was whisked about in play by first one side and then the other, but nearly always it ended by hurtling through the air for a point for the junior team.

During the rest period between the first and second halves the seniors declared themselves disgusted. The score was against them, and they had no hopes of pulling themselves up.

Lois had been sitting disconsolately by Beverly's side, gazing over the rows of faces of the spectators. Suddenly she grasped Beverly's arm in a heavy grip.

"Do you see what I see?" she demanded.

"What's that?" Caroline Johnson asked, overhearing Lois' remark.

"There—in the second row. See her—Shirley!"

"Come to gloat over us," responded Caroline bitterly. "A fine sport she is!"

"I wonder what happened to the scenes they were to take tonight?" Beverly murmured.

True enough, Shirley was in the stands watching her class team go down in ignominious defeat at the hands of the juniors. What the other girls did not know was that since their entrance to the gymnasium it had started in to rain and the picture scenes had been postponed. If she had known that the picture wouldn't be filmed tonight, she would have agreed to play, but as it was she had just entered before the ending of the first half. She saw the girls looking in her direction and guessed that they were talking about her. She knew what they were thinking, and in her heart she wished heartily that she had agreed to play. She wished that she had told Mr. Forsythe that she positively had to play tonight. She wished she had told him to take his old picture and go—— But what was the use? She had not responded to the girls' plea to aid her team, and consequently she must weather their scorn.

"I suppose she is laughing up her sleeve to think that without her the team is a flop," continued Lois indignantly.

"It would have been better if she had not come,"

agreed Caroline. "At least the girls would have thought more of her."

"We've got to do something about it," Beverly declared with vigor. "We've got to show her that the team is pretty good without her."

"We haven't a chance of winning," Lois said gloomily.

"Maybe we can't win," Beverly agreed quietly, "but we can at least show some spirit."

"It looked like a May dance last half," Caroline said dryly. "The girls were positively asleep on their feet."

"We've got to wake 'em up," Lois declared. "We'll show Miss Shirley Parker that the team can get along without her."

The referee's whistle blew shrilly, and the girls took their places on the floor. The juniors were swelled with pride. They had been a little fearful of the outcome of this game with the seniors, but now it was theirs. The smiles on their faces were smiles of triumph, and, almost unconsciously, they relaxed their rigid vigilance. It was the opportunity the seniors had been waiting for, and they seized it. The ball began going more often to pile up points for the seniors. The smiles slowly faded into surprise as the juniors watched their opponents coming to life. The spectators who had been gloomily watching their upper classmen going down in defeat brightened up amazingly and cheered lustily every time the ball hurtled toward the basket.

"Now their smiles are gone," the center whispered to Beverly with satisfaction as the seniors scored another point.

The ball whirled from Beverly's hands over the head of the junior guard to Lois and in another moment was in the basket. The score was evening rapidly. Now the seniors had caught the spirit of their captain and side center and were responding with vigor. They played as they had played when Shirley had been their leading light. They still had no hopes of winning, but at least they could make the score more even and defeat easier to endure.

The juniors began to worry. The game had seemed so surely theirs, and now there was a doubt creeping into it. The seniors had entered this second half with grim determination, and the juniors had not been prepared for it. But when the score began to even, they began to look to their laurels. Gradually they resumed the dash and fire with which they had played the first half of the game. They concentrated determinedly on each shot, and the ball went less and less often to the seniors now. Still the score kept mounting until the juniors were only one point ahead of the seniors.

The fans were jubilant. This basketball game was one that they would remember. Such a comeback as the seniors had made! Lois and Caroline, and even Beverly, cast more than one triumphant glance at Shirley. She fully realized, when she saw the smiles cast in her direction, that she was more or less responsible for the seniors' rise. She knew they had played so furiously because she was watching, in the hope that she would realize that after all she was not so important. She wished heartily that she had not come to the game. It would have been much better if she had stayed in her room.

The two teams fought furiously for the winning points, but they remained at a deadlock. The minutes were fleeting, and the end of the game was near. The seniors knew they could not win, but they still cherished the hope of tying the score. Finally the seniors won a free throw. Lois had the ball for the throw to the basket, and she cast an anxious eye about the gymnasium. A lot depended on her. If she made this basket the score would be tied. Her teammates whispered encouragement, and she flashed a glance up at the crowds, her glance singling out Shirley. Then she tossed to the basket and —missed! The game was over, and the seniors had lost.

Lois was in the depths of gloom. She had missed the biggest chance she had had.

"It's all right," Caroline said brightly. "We made a wonderful showing."

"It would have been better if we had tied the score," murmured Lois.

"But we played marvelously," Beverly said lightly. "We even surprised ourselves."

"Shirley would have made that free throw," Lois said heavily.

"Shirley!" Caroline scoffed. "She wouldn't even play. You at least did the best you could."

But Lois was not to be consoled. It irritated her to think that Shirley might have tied the score where she had failed. She knew Shirley was a better player than she was, but still it was disturbing. The girls had been good sports. Not one had said a word against her, even though she had failed to tie the score. Just the same, her indignation against Shirley grew by the minute.

CHAPTER IX

Fiction Dance

THE ENSUING DAYS were full of plans for the forthcoming Fiction Dance to be held in the gymnasium on Hallowe'en. It had come to a vote, and the girls had decided to have it a closed senior affair. The girls, as the name suggested, had to come dressed as a famous character from fiction, and they were busy preparing their costumes.

Shirley's antagonistic attitude had continued. She scarcely ever spoke to Beverly, and consistently avoided the rest of the Alpha members. She was deep in work on the film set, and the girls very seldom met her face to face on the campus. Lois, too, working on the picture, steadily kept away from Shirley and gave the red-headed girl no opportunity to cut her. When Shirley came back to her room she avoided Beverly's direct glance, and answered Beverly's questions in monosyllables.

Connie and her friends had not yet been inducted

into the Alpha Delta Sorority, and the girls were indefinite as to just when they would be. Shirley's declaration that she would resign from the group had rather dampened their interest in taking in new members. In fact, Shirley's declaration threatened to disrupt this group who had been friends for almost four years. They had no desire to lose one of their charter members, and yet with her present actions, Shirley was not keeping up her standard as a member.

Lenora, too, had informed Connie and her friends that they would have to do something to show that they were worthy of becoming members in the Alphas' distinguished society. The Alphas did not propose to initiate their new members, so that meant they would have to demonstrate their capabilities before they joined. What Connie and her friends might do was entirely up to them. The Alphas had put no limit on what their feat might be. It took a long while for Connie and the others to decide on what they would do, but once they had decided they went about with mischievous glints in their eyes and sly smiles that puzzled the Alphas.

Beverly, as president of the class, did more than her share of work with plans for the Fiction Dance. The gymnasium had to be decorated, an orchestra had to be procured, cards of admission for seniors only had to be printed. Of course, various committees were appointed to look after these tasks, but still last minute details and complications were referred to Beverly. Because she was so busy, Beverly had no time to think about Shirley and the differences in their relations. If she had had more time to herself, perhaps she would have worried over the change in Shirley. As it was, she felt hurt and sorry, but she could not let her thoughts dwell on it. Other occupations claimed her attention, and gradually she drifted away from thoughts of her one-time chum. She had become great friends with Connie Elwood, and it was with the latter and Lenora that she spent most of her precious spare moments.

The night of the dance came, clear and brilliant, with a star-studded sky. The brisk tang of late October was in the air, and the wind whistled gently through the falling leaves. The harvest moon was like a round yellow lantern in the sky, and early frost was nipping the pumpkins. The campus seemed a scene from a ghost story or fantastic play with strange figures, which were the girls in their costumes, flitting about in the moonlight.

The gymnasium was decorated lavishly with colored streamers, gayly colored autumn leaves, and yellow pumpkins that grinned on the scene of merriment with huge enjoyment. Dim, shaded lights threw their mellow tones over the kaleidoscope of dancers.

Captain Kidd was there in all his glory, dancing, incongruously enough, with Rip Van Winkle, while Robinson Crusoe whirled Peter Rabbit through the latest fox-trot. Joan of Arc joined the farce with Peter Pan, and David Copperfield glided over the floor with Sherlock Holmes. Not the least of the dancers were the freckle-faced Tom Sawyer and his friend Huckleberry Finn, together with Ivanhoe, the White Company, and other equally famous fiction characters. But there was one group that excited feverish interest. Clad in their traditional forest green, Robin Hood and five of his merry men frolicked in the midst of the other dancers. The noble forest men carried little bows, and their arrows were made of candy. They were most generous with the distribution of their "weapons," and all the dancers were accosted more than once by the little red darts.

At the halfway point in the evening's gayety the dancers unmasked, and there were surprised and amazed ejaculations as well as uproarious laughter.

"Lenora Whitehill! You would!" said Peter Pan, alias Lois, as she pounced on Sherlock Holmes.

Rosalie materialized from behind Joan of Arc's helmet, and Anne, as Robinson Crusoe, joined them.

"Where is Beverly and what is she?" asked Lois.

"As Sherlock Holmes, I can tell you," Lenora said. "She is Peter Rabbit."

"Here she comes," added Anne. "Beverly, your costume is ducky!"

"What happened to Robin Hood and his men?" Beverly asked.

The others looked about. The forest men had completely disappeared.

"That's funny," Rosalie murmured. "They were here a moment ago."

"They were here until we unmasked," Anne commented. "Where did they go?"

"Back to their forest," whispered Lenora dramatically.

"Here is a case for you," Lois said to her friend. "As Sherlock Holmes, you should be able to establish the identity of the mysterious Robin Hood and his merry men."

"Give me time, give me time," Lenora declaimed. "I, Sherlock Holmes, will bring the mystery to light."

"We don't want the mystery brought to light," Lois said. "We want it solved."

"I'll do that, too," Lenora promised. "But right now I'm thirsty. Let's visit the punch bowl."

"Do you think it could have been—Shirley?" Beverly asked slowly.

"And who else?" Lois demanded flippantly. "She hasn't five friends any more. Besides, she went to the movies again with Conway Grant."

"Then who——"

"I can't guess," Lois declared.

Nor could any of the rest of the masqueraders. Robin Hood and his men, with their little candy arrows, had stirred a mountain of interest, but no one could solve their identity. The forest men had danced and laughed and frolicked with the rest, and now they were a complete mystery. Where they had gone and how and when, the dancers could not tell. The orchestra swung into another popular melody, and the dancers drifted out onto the floor, and for a while the mystery of Robin Hood and his men was forgotten, but after the dance and on the following morning the campus talk was all of the vanished forest men.

The girls went through their classes, and afterward the Alphas, for the first time since the quarrel with Shirley, gathered in Beverly's room. Lenora had brought Connie along with her to the meeting, and the other Alphas wondered why.

"By the way, Sherlock Holmes," Lois said, "have you solved the mystery of the dance last night?"

"Ah," Lenora declaimed, "Sherlock Holmes is infallible. It is to solve the mystery that I called you all together."

"We are all burning up with curiosity," declared Rosalie.

"Yes, don't keep us in suspense," urged Lois. "Tell us."

"First of all," Lenora began, "I accuse Connie Elwood of knowing something about Robin Hood and his men."

"Connie!" the others echoed in surprise.

"Why do you accuse me?" Connie asked smiling.

"I've put two and two together," Lenora said wisely, "and I think you are Robin Hood."

"But the dance was only for seniors," interrupted Lois.

"Of course it was," echoed Connie.

"Just the same, you and your gang are responsible. Aren't you? Come now, confess!"

Connie laughed disarmingly. "I'll confess. We were the forest men."

"You were!" gasped Anne in amazement.

"We never thought it might be you," Rosalie murmured.

"How did you manage it?" Beverly wondered.

"Why did you do it?" asked Lois.

Connie held up a pleading hand. "One question at a time! Do you mean to say the stunt we played doesn't remind you of anything?"

The others looked mystified, and then Beverly laughed understandingly.

"Of course, the trick we played on the sopho-mores and juniors when we were freshmen."

Connie nodded. "Exactly. Lenora told us we would have to do something to—get us into the Alpha Deltas, so we took a page from the Alphas' own history. We heard of the prank you had played at a masquerade dance, and we decided to do some-thing similar."

Lenora shook Connie's hand solemnly. "You are now eligible for membership in our august body."

"But," Lois said suspiciously, "I don't see how Lenora guessed your identity."

"Easy." That individual waved aside the ques-tion. "I was in Weller's the other day and heard Kathleen order the candy arrows. Of course, at the time it didn't mean a thing to me, but last night I began to wonder. Then, when I remembered that all of your crowd disappeared immediately after dinner last night, I put two and two together."

"Marvelous!" murmured Lois.

"Elementary, my dear Lois, elementary," sighed Lenora.

Gradually the Alphas drifted to their own rooms until only Beverly and Connie were left.

"Beverly——"

"Yes?"

"Was—Shirley at the dance last night?" Connie asked.

"No." Beverly straightened the books on her desk and turned about. "Why do you ask?"

"I thought she would surely go with you," Connie said bluntly.

Beverly smiled ruefully. "She is—too busy with her picture work."

"You know that isn't so," Connie declared. "It would not have interfered last night. Has she quarreled with you?"

"Of course not."

"Beverly Gray, you aren't a bit good at fibbing!" Connie said. "Hasn't Shirley apologized for what she said the other day?"

"Was—it over me or my friends that the quarrel started?" Connie asked slowly.

"What makes you say a thing like that?" Beverly demanded.

"Well, I know Shirley doesn't like any of us, and I thought she might have objected to letting us become members of the Alpha Delta. Were we to blame?"

"No one was to blame," Beverly said staunchly. "Shirley has just been working too hard, and her nerves are on edge. Temperament, I guess you call it," she finished with a smile.

"But——"

"No buts about it. Shirley will be herself again when the picture is finished."

"Only if the picture is a failure," Connie said dryly. "That is the only thing that would bring her down to earth. If it is a success, people will begin patting her on the back, and she will be more conceited yet."

Beverly shook her head. "It is only a question of time. It is Shirley's first taste of success. Naturally, it will go to her head, but not for long. Shirley will get over it."

"I wish I thought so," Connie said sighing. "You don't suppose it would do any good if I talked to her about apologizing——"

"The best thing you can do is to let her alone," Beverly interrupted. "If we try to influence her, it will only make her angry. Let's just leave things as they are and see what happens."

CHAPTER X

Holidays

THE GAY COLORS of autumn faded, and the bleakness of gray winter descended on the campus. Frost blackened the trees and painted pictures on room windows. Icicles hung from the roofs of the dormitory houses, and the girls wasted little time outdoors unless they were engaged in some sport.

The Christmas holidays came, and with them the midwinter vacation. The girls separated, each to spend the holidays at home. Half the term was over, and when they gathered again at Vernon, it would be on the last stretch of their college days.

In the last days before the Christmas holidays, Shirley had not changed. Production on the picture had been held up because the leading man had contracted a heavy cold, and now it would not go forward until after the holidays. Mr. Forsythe planned to have the picture finished early in February, if there were no more interruptions. Shirley, the director admitted, was indeed a splendid actress. Undoubtedly she would prove a find for the cinema world. He was already planning for her to go to Hollywood with him.

Lois, working on the set with Shirley, brought back different tales, though. She did not praise Shirley or her acting. She told of the slights and contempt Shirley showered on those about her. It seemed as though Beverly had been totally wrong when she said Shirley would get over it. Shirley hadn't. Every day she drew farther away from those who used to be her friends.

Beverly rose and threw another log on the fire. Yesterday afternoon she and Anne had arrived in Renville for the holidays. She sank back in her easy chair before the roaring fire in the grate and let her eyes seek out pictures formed by the dancing flames. Shadows flickered on walls and ceiling of the Gray living room. In one corner stood a giant spruce tree already decked with its festive trimming, for tonight was Christmas Eve. Beverly's fingers played an aimless tattoo on the chair arm, in time with the dance music that came through the loud speaker of the radio. Her parents had gone out a few minutes before, and she was waiting for the Lucky Circle to arrive.

Somehow a warm fire always made her dreamy. The flames, as they leaped and died down and leaped high again, seemed to form pictures. It was strange that she was feeling lonely tonight, Christmas Eve, when all the world was gay and merrymaking. Last Christmas Eve Shirley had been here with her in Renville, and the Lucky Circle had taken the red-headed girl into their midst as an honorary member. Then, too, Jim Stanton was haunting her thoughts tonight. It was over a year since she had seen him, and she wondered where he was, if he was happy, if he was celebrating Christmas as was the rest of the world. What was it like out in Wyoming, where he was? She knew in the northwest of the state is found Yellowstone National Park, and there were a lot of cattle ranches in the country thereabout, but beyond that her knowledge of the West was limited.

Last year this time she and Shirley had been the best of friends, and now they were almost strangers. She felt an almost irresistible longing for an old friend, such as Jim or Shirley used to be, to welcome Christmas Day with. But Jim was hundreds of miles away, and Shirley—— Of course, all the boys and girls in the Lucky Circle were her friends, and she felt affection for each one of them, yet she wanted someone especially her own tonight.

She walked to the window and looked out over the garden. It had started snowing late in the afternoon, and already the trees and flower bushes were

covered with a white blanket. From the window
she went to the dining room and surveyed the table,
laden with goodies for a midnight lunch. The
Lucky Circle was to go caroling and would return
to the Gray home for sandwiches and hot drinks.
Experimentally she tasted a portion of the chocolate cake. Her mother always made delicious chocolate cake.

The doorbell echoed through the house, and she
cast an anxious eye at the clock. Probably the
Lucky Circle, but they were early. It was only
eight-fifteen. She threw open the door and stood
'still in surprise.

The tall, bronzed young man who stood there,
his white teeth flashing in a wide smile, and his gray
eyes alight, did not in any way resemble the six
joyous members of the Lucky Circle that she had
expected.

"Jim!" Beverly cried joyfully.

"No other," he declared and enveloped her in a
bear hug. "Merry Christmas!"

"Merry Christmas yourself," she retorted smilingly, breathlessly disentangling herself from his
strong arms and patting her disarranged curls.
"Take your things off and come into the living
room and let me look at you," she commanded.

"Anything to please," he laughed softly. "I'm
going to do a lot of looking myself."

"You're looking fine," Beverly declared as they stood before the fire. "So tan——"

"Result of the sun and the open air," he said.

"—And healthy, and big and powerful——"

"Do I look good to you?" he asked in a low tone.

"So good!" she declared. "I was feeling rather blue this evening before you came."

"Blue!" he echoed. "On Christmas Eve? Where is that cheerful organization known as the Lucky Circle?"

"They're——" The doorbell cut short her answer. "There they are now. Do they know you are home?"

"No," he answered. "I got in town just before dinner. I haven't been any place but home. I've seen none of them."

"Then let's surprise them," Beverly said breathlessly. She pushed him into the dining room as another impatient peal at the doorbell sounded. "Stay in there until I give you the signal, and don't you dare eat the chocolate cake! Coming!" She called this last as the doorbell was rung again.

"We were just about to walk in," Boyd announced as Beverly opened the door.

"We thought you weren't home or had died or something," added Joan Roberts.

"I—I was in the kitchen," Beverly answered.

"Take off your things, everybody, and come into the living room."

"Golly, that fire feels good!" declared Tommy Chandler as he and Gordon Brewster took up their stand before it. "It's going to be cold to carol tonight."

"I've got a fine lunch fixed up for afterward," said Beverly.

"Let's eat it now," Boyd suggested shamelessly.

A chorus of teasing and chatter greeted Boyd's proposal.

"Have you heard from Jim lately, Beverly?" Barbara West asked.

Beverly smiled. "Yes, I heard from him today."

"I wish he could be home for Christmas," Tommy murmured.

Beverly seized the opportunity. "Why don't you rub your magic lamp and tell your wish to a genie?" she asked gayly.

"Find me a genie," retorted Tommy.

"Tell it to me," Beverly proposed. "I'm not a genie, but maybe I can do something about your wish."

"Are you going to fly to Wyoming and bring him back with you?" Anne asked interestedly.

"I don't have to," Beverly said, going into the dining room and coming out again proudly with her visitor in tow, "because he is already here."

The young people gave Jim a welcome that made up for the months he had spent away from them all. They shook his hand and patted him on the shoulder until he declared himself worn out from the exertion.

For a short while the young people danced, and then they donned their coats and hats and went out with their song sheets. It was snowing, and the sky overhead was clouded, and there was no sign of the moon or stars. The eight young people slowly made their way from one home to another, their voices raised in carols.

As her clear, rich contralto mingled with the tones of the others, Beverly realized that all her former depression had disappeared. She flashed a glance at Jim, who had her hand firmly imprisoned in his, and flushed at the ardent light in his eyes. Ever since he had come back earlier in the evening, she felt that he was different. He had gone away scarcely more than a boy fresh from college, and he had come back a young man, with a man's purpose and determination. She looked across at Anne who was standing beside Tommy Chandler, and noticed the rapt expression on both young faces. The two were floating in a paradise all their own, and Beverly felt a faint stirring in her heart. Since they had gone to college, she had really grown a little apart from Anne. She determined then and there

that she would immediately try to regain her old
footing with her chum. She had never supposed for
a moment that Anne and Tommy——

"Happy?" Jim whispered in her ear.

She flashed him a starry glance and nodded. Disturbing thoughts of Shirley had been banished,
leaving nothing but gladness and an infinite peace
in her heart. The snow was sifting gently down,
and the lights from the homes sent out warmth and
cheer to the singers. Wreaths and candles were hung
in windows, while trees were decorated with gar-
lands gay, and tiny stockings were filled with
goodies. The choristers finished "O Little Town of
Bethlehem" and started on their final song. Their
voices rang clear and mellow through the still night
as they wound their way back to the Gray home.

The lunch Beverly had prepared disappeared
with amazing rapidity once the eight hungry Lucky
Circle members descended on it. Over their sandwiches and chocolate the young people talked and
talked. They had been separated long, and now
they chatted to their hearts' content. Confidences
were exchanged and plans talked over. Only those
who have been absent for a long time from their
friends know how dear a reunion can be. Jim,
especially, felt the friendliness and good comrade-
ship that was present. He who had been absent for

so many months was thankful that at last he was back with old friends.

After the young people had devoured everything edible, and the hands on the clock had spun around alarmingly fast, they departed for a few precious hours' sleep before the dawning of Christmas Day. Jim, however, lingered after the others, and Beverly drew him into the living room.

"Let's have an old-fashioned talk, Jim," she proposed, pushing him into the comfortable chair before the fireplace and kneeling on a cushion at his feet. "I'm not a bit sleepy yet."

"At your service, lady," Jim laughed.

"Tell me about Wyoming. Is the bridge finished?"

"Yes. I'm finished with that job. I have orders to go to New York to confer with another engineer on another job, but I shall be in Vernon for your commencement."

"Commencement!" Beverly smiled. "It doesn't seem possible that I've almost finished with school days."

"Sorry?"

She nodded. "Isn't one always sorry to find out she is grown up at last? I shall miss the girls a lot."

He leaned forward until his gray eyes encountered her blue ones. "Are you really grown up, Beverly?"

"Do I act as though I were still in kindergarten?" she laughed.

He smiled and then became serious again. "I mean—oh, Beverly! You must know what I want to say, what I've come hundreds of miles to tell you. I love you and I want you to marry me. Will you?"

"Jim!" she gasped. The thought that Jim might feel any more than friendliness for her had never entered her mind. She had never realized that out of their lifelong friendship something new and beautiful might spring.

"Have I spoken too soon?" he asked gently. "I didn't mean to startle you. I thought you realized that now we both are really and truly grown up with most of our lives before us. What do you say, Beverly? Is it—yes?"

"I don't know, Jim," Beverly said confusedly. "I like you, but——"

"You don't love me. Is that it?"

"N-not in that way. I've never thought of you in any way but as a friend, a chum I could trust."

"You can always trust me, Beverly, you know that, don't you?" he asked searchingly.

She nodded. "But now I feel as if my world had suddenly turned topsy-turvy. You must give me time to find myself."

"I'll wait, Beverly," Jim said softly. "I'll wait forever if need be. Perhaps some day——"

"Perhaps some day," she agreed reluctantly. "But now—— I'm not out of school yet. I've so many plans and hopes for the future. I want a career. I want to do something—I don't think I could be content if I settled down now and threw all those dreams aside. They would be bound to creep in and mar the most perfect happiness."

"Nothing can mar true happiness," he said gravely. "Even a career cannot make up for everything."

Beverly thought suddenly of another young man who had said almost the same thing to her many months ago. Larry Owens, the Secret Service agent, had said that some day she would find that love could make up for all the things she thought she wanted now. Here was Jim telling her almost the same thing. Was it true?

"Perhaps not," she admitted. "But I'm afraid I'll have to find that out for myself. I don't know whether I love you or not. I've never thought about it," she said frankly. "There, I hurt you when I said that. I'm sorry, Jim."

He patted her hand and stood up. "I'm glad you told me, anyway. I hope you have success in your career, and if I can help in any way, you know I will."

"Then you aren't—angry?"

"Angry? Of course not! Let's go on being pals for now, shall we?" he asked smiling.

She nodded and slipped her hand into his. "That's the Jim I know."

When the door closed behind him she turned and went slowly up to her room. She knelt for a long time looking out at the snow. She hadn't wanted to hurt Jim, and yet she had. She didn't want to marry, at least, not for a while yet. She had always thought of marriage as something in the far and distant future. She wanted a career. She wanted to make some of her dreams come true. She sighed and turned to the bed. Life was complicated.

During the days of her vacation the Lucky Circle frolicked in the snow with skiing, coasting, ice skating; they held parties and dances, and in all of them Beverly joined heartily. Yet whenever she encountered Jim's gaze a restraint fell on her that she could not break. She could no longer consider him the laughing playmate that he had always been. No more could she ride and laugh and dance with him as unconsciously as she had done in other years. Always there was a feeling of difference between them, and it showed in little things she said and did.

If Beverly's parents guessed that there was anything wrong with their daughter they gave no sign of it. It never occurred to them to force their questions or their advice on Beverly. When she wanted their confidence she would seek them out, and they knew that. They had confidence in their daughter's ability to solve her own problems sanely, but they were willing to help her should she ask them to. Until she did so, they would not interfere with her affairs.

Jim had never again said a word of what he and Beverly had discussed on Christmas Eve. He didn't have to. She was acutely aware of his every glance and word. Words and actions that she had scarcely noticed before took on a new meaning.

She almost welcomed the day when it was time to return to Vernon. She hated to leave her parents and friends of the Lucky Circle, but now she would have a little peace. She could forget she was grown up and for a little while laugh and act as a girl again. One simply couldn't be dignified and serious around the effervescent Lenora and Lois. Then, too, she would have time to herself to think and to plan for the future. Perhaps, after graduation, when she came back to Renville, Jim would have forgotten all about this proposal, and they could again be the jolly friends they had been.

CHAPTER XI

Rivals

COLLEGE was in session again, and the dormitory houses were alive with gay young things that dashed here and there swinging books, regardless of the danger of spilling them all. During social hour voices were lifted in college songs, to the accompaniment of a piano or ukulele, or sometimes to no accompaniment at all. Mid-year exams were over, and the girls devoted their leisure time now to pleasures. Weller's had again become the center of attraction after afternoon classes, and many studies and mischievous plans were discussed over the shiny table tops.

Beverly, upon her return, had thrown herself into senior activities with a whirl. Plans were under way to make this last half of the senior term memorable to each girl in the class. A dance was planned for the end of the term, and bids were being sought for a suitable ballroom. Then, too, the

girls planned a dinner to be given on Class Day instead of the usual play that was a symbol of the
day. All these things Beverly was vitally interested
in, and she gave her attention to every little detail
that came up. Nothing was too much trouble for
her. She listened patiently to everything anyone
had to say. The other girls wondered how she managed to get so much done in the little spare time
she had.

Beverly had encountered Shirley almost the moment she set foot inside her room on her return.

"Hello," Beverly had started in an attempt to
become friends. When Shirley responded ungra-
ciously she continued: "The Lucky Circle all sent
you their regards."

"Thanks," Shirley said laconically. "It was nice
of them," she said coolly and left the room.

That was all. Ever since then the two had
scarcely spoken more than ten words. The situation
now reminded Beverly of their first term together.
Then they had lived and studied and slept in the
same room without speaking. Why Shirley should
constantly go around seeking a quarrel was a mystery to Beverly. She had done her best to get back
on friendly footing with the red-headed girl, but
Shirley would not respond, and Beverly's pride now
would not let her make any more overtures, only
to be snubbed.

Anne, since the girls' return, went about with a quiet happiness and dreamy expression that puzzled the other girls. When gayly teased about her contentment she merely smiled quietly and gave them no satisfaction whatever as to the cause of her joy. She left them all guessing. Even Lois could not fathom the mystery of her roommate.

Lois brought to the Alpha members news from the moving-picture set. The picture was fast nearing completion, but lately things had started happening that puzzled even Mr. Forsythe.

"What sort of things?" Lenora asked when Lois told the Alpha Delta members about it.

"Well, for one thing, a camera was mysteriously smashed the other day," Lois answered.

"Nothing mysterious about that," Lenora commented dryly. "Evidently somebody was careless and——"

"Nobody on the set did it. At least, no one admits it," Lois interrupted. "One day, when work ended, the camera was all right, and the next morning it was smashed completely."

"Ah," murmured Lenora dramatically. "Mystery on the campus! Who Smashed the Camera, or Who Walks in Her Sleep?"

"Hush," Rosalie laughingly admonished her roommate. "Doesn't anyone know who did it?" she asked Lois.

Lois shook her head. "Mr. Forsythe suspects it might be somebody from Cordial Pictures Company prowling about trying to stop production on the picture. Did you know the Cordial Pictures made Miss Wilder a handsome offer if she would put the Forsythe Film Company off the campus and let Cordial make a picture here?"

"Aha!" Lenora declaimed. "Rivals!"

"It looks like it," Beverly laughed. "Tell us more, Lois. We haven't had anything interesting to happen this term."

"I also heard," Lois leaned closer, and three heads were immediately bent attentively, "that they had made an offer to Shirley to go to Hollywood."

"They took Marcia Lyman away from Forsythe Films, so they thought they could get Shirley too," Beverly murmured.

"Did Shirley accept?" Rosalie asked.

"She couldn't have done so," Lois answered. "She is still working on the picture."

"Evidently she still retains some mistaken sense of honor," drawled Lenora. "Oh, I'm sorry," she said slowly as Beverly flashed her a glance. "I forget you still consider her a friend of yours."

"Not exactly a friend," Beverly admitted dryly.

"My blood boils every time I see Shirley," Lois declared. "That girl is so satisfied with herself she

doesn't consider anyone else's feelings at all. Why,
the other day——"

"Tell us about these mysterious rivals," Beverly
interrupted calmly. She had no desire to listen to
any account of Shirley's shortcomings.

Lois took the hint and changed the subject.
"That is all I know about them," she admitted.
"But if they stay in Vernon, some excitement is
bound to develop."

"Three cheers," declared Lenora. "I don't mind
admitting that I was getting a little bored, things
have been so quiet."

"Why don't you start something?" demanded
Lois.

"I can't," grieved Lenora. "I'm a senior and have
to be good no matter how much it hurts."

"I'll wager it hurts a lot," grinned Lois. "You
were never cut out to be good. You——"

"No insults," warned Lenora. "I shall have to use
drastic measures if you ruffle my senior dignity!"

"Let's go to Weller's," suggested Beverly. "I
haven't been there for over a week, and now that
I have an hour of leisure I want to put it to good
use."

"I'm with you!" Lenora declared enthusiastically.

"I'm going over to see if Anne is through in the
library," Lois answered.

"And I promised to pay a visit to Connie and help her with her French," said Rosalie.

"Then we shall fare forth alone," said Lenora gayly, linking an arm within Beverly's and leading her from the room and out of the Hall.

The girls strolled slowly along College Avenue talking aimlessly, and as they came into Vernon, stopped to look into shop windows. They made trifling purchases in several small shops before they went to Weller's. When they left the ice-cream saloon it was late, and early February twilight was settling down. They were passing the private railway coach of the Forsythe Film Company when Lenora grasped Beverly's arm and pulled her into the shadow of a tree.

"Look!" she whispered.

Work on the picture had long since finished for the day, and the material had been stored in the railway coach for the night. Mr. Forsythe and the other people had no doubt returned to the hotel where they were staying while Shirley went to the Hall for dinner. The railway coach was deserted, or it should have been.

The two seniors, watching breathlessly, saw a man hurl a stone through one of the car windows and heard the tinkle of glass.

"What do you suppose he is doing that for?" Lenora whispered excitedly.

"So he can climb in the window," answered Beverly.

"He's too fat," murmured Lenora. "He can't climb in that little window. He will get stuck."

Beverly laughed. "Do you think he is one of the rivals?"

"Of course," said Lenora. "If he belonged to the Forsythe Company, he wouldn't have to climb in the window."

The man had placed a box beneath the window. He climbed upon this and succeeded in pulling himself up to the window. There, halfway in and halfway out, he remained. He made a grotesque figure as he squirmed and fought to pull himself clear. His legs waved in the air fantastically.

"What did I tell you?" Lenora giggled. "He is stuck. He looks like a spider."

"What shall we do?" Beverly asked, laughing.

"We'll rescue him," said Lenora.

CHAPTER XII

Stolen Film

THE TWO GIRLS crept forward, and as they came nearer they could hear the man puffing and groaning to himself.

"Stop kicking and we'll pull you out," shouted Lenora.

Immediately the two legs became still. Each girl grabbed one and pulled with all her might. The man came free of the window, and much quicker than the three of them had expected. He fell flat on his face in the dust of the road while the two girls went stumbling backward.

"Why didn't you take care?" the man roared, wiping the dust from his face, red with his recent exertion.

"We might have let you stick there," retorted Lenora. "How did we know you would come out so easily?"

117

"Well, thanks, anyway," he said, rubbing his legs stiffly.

"What were you trying to crawl through the window for?" demanded Lenora.

"Because the door is locked," he said dryly.

"No!" murmured Lenora in mock surprise.

"You aren't by any chance on the staff of Cordial Pictures Company?" asked Beverly.

"Never heard of them," retorted the man. "Thanks again," he said, nonchalantly straightening his tie and starting off toward the town.

"He is nothing if not abrupt," said Lenora. "Let's follow him."

"Why?" Beverly demanded. "He probably expects us to and will lead us on a wild-goose chase."

"We'll follow him anyway," Lenora said, pulling Beverly along with her. "What do you suppose he wanted?"

"I wonder," Beverly murmured.

They kept their quarry in sight and hurried along the streets. The man headed for the very center of the town. When he hurried his steps, the girls too increased their speed, always keeping him a few paces ahead of them. At the entrance to the Wildon Hotel he paused, glanced about him, then hurried into the building.

"I suppose that is where he is staying," commented Lenora.

"Our mystery that wasn't a mystery," laughed Beverly. "We suspected him of dire plans against the Forsythe Film Company, and he is probably only an innocent visitor to the town. I guess he tried to get into the private car just for curiosity."

"I refuse to believe our mystery has fizzled out," declared Lenora. "I didn't like his looks."

"Well, whether you did or not," Beverly continued, "we had better rush back to Chadwick Hall, or we shall miss dinner."

"Goodness me," cried Lenora, "that would be a tragedy! Especially when I am so hungry. Pulling people from car windows is appetizing work."

The next afternoon Lenora was in Beverly's room discussing the latest plans for the senior dance when Lois burst in upon them.

"Gracious, why don't you knock?" complained Lenora. "You will give us heart failure, popping in on us that way."

"I've got news," gasped Lois, dropping on the bed beside Lenora.

"Has somebody been murdered?" asked Beverly.

"No, but——"

"Take your time, take your time," cautioned Lenora. "You stutter when you talk fast."

"I do not," defended Lois. "If you don't want to hear my news I won't tell you."

"Of course we want to hear it," Beverly assured her. "Lenora was teasing you."

"Come on, tell us," urged Lenora.

"I don't know whether I shall," declared Lois loftily. "You don't appreciate what a news gatherer I am. Here the very minute I hear something I rush to tell you, and you———"

Lenora raised a cushion threateningly. "Are you going to tell us?"

Lois' indignation suddenly evaporated, and she smiled. "Somebody stole three rolls of film from the company's private railway coach last night," she announced.

Lenora and Beverly exchanged glances. "Somebody what?" they demanded simultaneously.

"Some unknown person, male or female, feloniously———" began Lois when Lenora interrupted.

"Speak English," she directed.

"All right," Lois grinned. "Somebody took three rolls of film from the railway coach."

"How did the thief get into the car?" Beverly asked.

"The door was broken open," explained Lois, "and there was also a window smashed."

Lenora laughed. "We know about that."

"You do?" Lois said in surprise. "How?"

"We'll tell you later." Lenora waved aside the

query. "Is Mr. Forsythe worried over the stolen film?"

"I'll say he is," declared Lois. "He has threatened to go back to Hollywood tomorrow and give up trying to film this picture. Something is always interrupting his plans. He believes someone working for Cordial Pictures took this film as a last desperate effort to wreck his plans for a college picture."

"Can't he find the thief and get the film back?" Beverly asked.

"He says whoever took it has probably destroyed it by now," replied Lois. "He also says he has spent too much money already on this picture, and he won't make it over. If the film isn't recovered before tomorrow night he is going back to Hollywood and give the whole thing up."

"What a shame!" Lenora cried. "Then we won't get the indoor swimming pool."

"It rather looks as though we won't," agreed Lois.

"Hasn't he any idea at all who the thief might be?" Beverly wanted to know.

"He is completely in the dark," Lois answered. "One thing, we know the thief couldn't have left town by train today because a split rail has held up all trains for hours."

Lenora snapped her fingers suddenly and, grab-

bing Beverly by the arm, pulled her to the door, at
the same time shouting over her shoulder at Lois:

"Go back to Mr. Forsythe and tell him to hold
everything. The Alphas are on the trail of the film,
and we will recover it for him."

"B-but——" began Lois, taken by surprise,
"how are you——"

"Our methods are deep and mysterious," retorted Lenora laughingly, "but we never acknowledge defeat. Sherlock Holmes never fails!"

CHAPTER XIII

Recovery

LENORA pulled Beverly along with her and left Lois gazing after them in complete bewilderment.

"Just a minute!" Beverly stopped firmly in the living room. "Where are we going, might I ask?"

"Of course you might ask," said Lenora magnanimously. "We're going to catch the thief and return the film to Mr. Forsythe."

"But where are we going to get it?" Beverly asked patiently.

"Have you forgotten the man we pulled out of the car window yesterday?" demanded Lenora. "Isn't it more than likely that he is the thief?"

"Granted," acknowledged Beverly.

"And didn't we see him go into the Wildon Hotel?" continued Lenora.

"Yes," Beverly admitted.

"Then we will go there after him," Lenora said. "It is all very simple."

"Suppose he isn't there any more," Beverly suggested. "We don't know his name, we don't know what room he has, we——"

"Don't be so pessimistic," Lenora groaned. "Come along and trust to luck."

The two girls almost ran into town to the hotel. It was only when they were within sight of the steps leading into the building that they slowed their pace.

"What do we do now, Sherlock?" demanded Beverly.

"Let's go into the lobby," Lenora suggested. "Perhaps we can see the mysterious rival."

Lady Luck must have been in one of her most generous moods, for as the girls entered the lobby, Lenora collided squarely with the man they were looking for. He was in a hurry and rushed from them out onto the street before the girls were aware that it had really been he. Then Lenora hailed a bellboy.

"Who was that man?" she asked.

"He's registered as Mr. Smith," the boy answered.

"Thanks," said Lenora.

"That doesn't tell us much," Beverly smiled. "There are thousands of 'Smiths' in the world."

"Probably an assumed name," agreed Lenora.

"We have to do something, but what? Just thinking about his name won't help us."

"You tell me what to do," Beverly suggested. "You are playing Sherlock Holmes."

"Watch me!"

Lenora marched up to the desk and confronted the clerk. "What is Mr. Smith's room number?" she asked with her most bewitching smile.

The clerk proved to have no resistance against such magnetic personality and responded promptly, "Four hundred and two."

"Thank you."

"Now what?" demanded Beverly.

"We are going up to room 402," announced Lenora, heading for the elevator.

"B-but——" began Beverly.

"No buts!" Lenora said firmly. "Are you coming, or do I go by myself?"

"I'm coming," Beverly said promptly. "But are you crazy? We won't be able to get into his room. It will probably be locked."

"We've got to get that film," said Lenora determinedly. "Vernon needs an indoor swimming pool," she added laughingly.

"But we aren't even sure that he has it," Beverly said.

"We'll find out," Lenora declared.

The elevator drew up to the fourth floor, and the two girls stepped out. As the iron grille clanged shut behind them Lenora turned to the right.

"There it is—402."

"Are you going to knock on the door?" Beverly asked.

"We just saw him go out, didn't we?" Lenora answered.

"He might have friends," said Beverly calmly.

"Right you are. We'll knock," said Lenora.

They knocked several times, but there was no response. Lenora turned the doorknob, but the door was locked.

"Tsk, tsk," she said. "Foiled!"

Beverly meanwhile had been looking about the hall. She came up to Lenora with three keys in her hand.

"What are they?" Lenora asked in surprise.

"Well, if we are going to commit robbery," Beverly laughed, "we might as well do it in style. I took these keys from empty rooms. Try them."

Lenora seized them and one after the other fitted them in the lock, but the door did not yield. Beverly replaced the keys in the doors from which she had taken them, and the two girls conferred.

"We can't climb through the keyhole," Lenora sighed. "Even the transom is too small. What will we do?"

Beverly snapped her fingers. "I know! Maybe there is a fire escape!"

"Brilliant idea," Lenora declared.

"The room next to this is empty, we can get out on the fire escape from there," Beverly proposed.

"If there is one," Lenora added.

"It would be funny, wouldn't it," Beverly laughed, "if after all this trouble we were on the wrong track? Mr. Smith might prove to be only a harmless traveling salesman."

"It would be a tragedy," Lenora groaned. "Sherlock Holmes would be disgraced!"

The two girls entered the next room and noiselessly went to the window. They were in luck. There was a fire escape outside this room and the next. They raised the window and in a moment were out and at the window to the next room.

"It's stuck," groaned Lenora, hammering along the pane. "I never saw a hotel window that didn't stick."

"Maybe it's locked," suggested Beverly.

"No, you can see that the catch is turned. I'll bet it hasn't been opened for years," Lenora declared, pushing and hammering again.

"Get your fingers along the edge, and we will both push *together*," directed Beverly.

The two girls managed to move the window with only dirt and minor injuries to their fingers.

As quietly as possible the two climbed into the room and looked around.

"Where would he keep the films?" whispered Lenora.

"You are asking me," retorted Beverly. "He might have already destroyed them, you know."

"Let's hope he didn't," murmured Lenora. "Look, there is his suitcase."

"They might be in there," Beverly agreed.

Lenora opened the traveling bag, but there was nothing of interest to them to be found. She replaced the bag, and they continued with their search. Lenora was bent over looking under the bed and she nearly collapsed from fright when the telephone rang.

"Gosh, that scared me!" she murmured, her hand on the receiver.

"Don't answer it," Beverly cautioned. "The room is supposed to be empty. Mr. Smith is out."

"That's right! It would have gotten us in trouble, wouldn't it?" Lenora murmured. "Oh, keep quiet!" she said irritably as the bell rang again.

"Look, Lenora!"

Beverly had opened the closet and far back in one corner she had come upon three black boxes piled together. She dragged one out to the light and opened it.

"The film!" cried Lenora. "We have saved the day!"

"Let's take them and get out," Beverly said quickly.

The girls had just picked up the three precious boxes of film when loud voices sounded in the hall.

"I'm sure they came into this room," one voice said. "I got a good look at them as they stood on the fire escape fussing with the window."

"They are after us," whispered Lenora.

"Come!"

The two climbed out the window and reached the safety of the next room just as the door to Mr. Smith's room was thrown open. Lenora pressed her ear to the partition between the rooms and listened intently. The two couldn't go out into the hall for they would surely be seen and recognized. If they went out by the fire escape they would also be seen.

"They are going to search the whole floor," Lenora reported from her listening post. "What will we do?"

"Get under the bed," Beverly urged. "They might not look there."

The two crawled under the bed and waited breathlessly to be discovered. Two men entered the room and looked about. They looked in the closet and everywhere but under the bed. Right at the most particular moment Lenora was seized with an overwhelming desire to sneeze. The floor was covered with dust, and she had inhaled it. It was not a short, quick sneeze, but long and shuddering, not completely muffled by Beverly's admonishing hand.

"What was that?" one of the men said quickly.

"Somebody sneezing," his companion answered. "Out in the hall, I guess."

"Well, we might as well look farther," the first man spoke again. "There is nothing in here."

"Thank your lucky stars," Beverly whispered to her friend. "I don't see what angel prompted them to think that sneeze was out in the hall!"

"I wonder if anyone ever sweeps these floors," Lenora murmured, wrinkling her nose distastefully.

"Don't sneeze any more," Beverly begged. "If you do, we will surely be discovered."

"I can't help it," Lenora groaned. "What am I supposed to do when my nose tickles?"

"Swallow it," Beverly said briefly.

"What? My nose?" Lenora demanded.

Beverly laughed. "No, silly. The sneeze. Shshsh! Someone is coming!"

Footsteps came along the hall, paused at the door, and then went on into the next room.

"Mr. Smith, I reckon," murmured Lenora. "I

wish the excitement would die down so we could get away. I'm tired of lying on the floor."

"Not any more so than I," declared Beverly. "This whole thing was your idea."

"I didn't suggest getting under the bed," Lenora retorted. "Besides, we got the films, didn't we?"

"Yes, and we might be arrested as burglars," answered Beverly.

Lenora wrinkled her nose in disgust as the dust stirred. "Home was never like this," she declared. "Let's take a chance and get out from under here."

The floor boards squeaked protestingly as the two struggled out from under the bed, and they held their breath lest someone enter the room and discover them. Lenora pressed her ear to the wall and listened intently.

"Looks as though everybody has gone out," she said thankfully.

"But how are we to get out?" Beverly demanded. "We can't go out and through the lobby as we entered."

"Why not?" Lenora asked innocently.

"Mr. Smith will be waiting for us, to claim his films, won't he?" asked Beverly. "We shall have to use the fire escape."

"Someone might be looking for us that way too," frowned Lenora.

"We'll have to chance it," said Beverly firmly. "Let's get going."

"A good thing it is almost dark," declared Lenora. "Someone from the ground won't see us as quickly as if it were broad daylight."

"Don't make so much noise," Beverly warned as Lenora's high heels clicked on the iron ladder-like steps.

"I can't help it," Lenora said plaintively. "I'll never take up burglaring as a profession."

"Crime does not pay," Beverly reminded her, laughing. "Your detective stunt isn't so good either."

"At least we have the films," Lenora said with satisfaction. "Won't Mr. Forsythe be surprised!"

"It saves him a lot of money," Beverly agreed.

"And, incidentally, Shirley will have her big chance after all," finished Lenora critically.

"What do you mean 'will have'?" demanded Beverly. "She has had it."

"If the picture wasn't shown, what good would her chance do her?" Lenora asked. "We are doing her a good turn by returning the films."

"That's so," Beverly admitted. "It never occurred to me that——"

"There they go," a voice rang out above them.

"Our escape is discovered," Lenora said dramatically. "We better run."

"The faster the better," rejoined Beverly.

The two clattered down the rest of the steps, and voices rang out behind them, challenging them to halt. At the bottom of the fire escape the two broke into a run, cutting through the alley in back of the hotel. Their pursuers were close on their heels.

"Hide in here," Beverly gasped, pulling Lenora into a little shack in the back yard of a dry goods store.

The girls stood in the darkness, scarcely breathing, while the two men who had been chasing them dashed past in hot pursuit.

"Whew!" sighed Lenora weakly. "That was a narrow escape."

"We aren't safe yet," declared Beverly. "They might come back this way."

The two men did return through the alleyway. For several minutes they stood before the shack in which the two girls waited nervously.

"I can't understand how they got away so quickly," the one man declared, glancing up and down the alley.

Lenora nudged Beverly gleefully, her face wreathed in triumphant smiles. The men were so close that they might have touched them, and yet they had not discovered the girls.

After a moment the men proceeded on their way

and reëntered the hotel. It was then that the girls ventured from their hiding place, to leave the alley. Sedately carrying the three boxes of film, the two walked to the railway coach of the film company and laid the films before Mr. Forsythe.

"Where in the world have you been?" Lois demanded when the two appeared. "You are all smudged with dust."

"That's what comes from hiding under beds," laughed Beverly.

"Hiding under beds!" echoed Mr. Forsythe. "What do you mean?"

"It's a long story," Lenora said dramatically. Then with true dramatic zeal, she proceeded to tell the events of their playing detective. She was at the height of her glory when she had a spellbound audience before her, and now she made the most of her opportunity to play heroine.

The next afternoon Lenora and Lois burst in upon Beverly, the former waving a newspaper high in the air.

"Beverly! We're in the paper!" gleefully shouted Lenora. "At last the tale of our desperate deeds has broken into print."

"They don't even mention you," said Lois dryly.

"It is us," insisted Lenora. "They couldn't mean anybody else."

"Is it or isn't it, and what is it?" demanded Beverly laughing.

"Listen," Lenora said, "I'll read you what it says. 'Yesterday afternoon two thieves, believed to be young women, broke into a room in the Hotel Wildon by means of the fire escape. They were seen from the ground, but by the time the hotel authorities reached the room in question the two had disappeared. Nothing of great value was stolen.' It means us, doesn't it?" Lenora asked.

"It sounds like us," Beverly admitted. "It doesn't say anything of them chasing us down the fire escape."

"They must have left that part out," murmured Lois.

"Evidently Mr. Smith didn't tell them what we took," continued Lenora. "The article says nothing of great value."

"Mr. Forsythe sent two of his assistants down to the hotel to see Mr. Smith last night," Lois contributed, "but he had already checked out."

"Maybe he thought we would send the police for him," said Lenora.

"Another thing," Lois said. "In appreciation of your returning the stolen films, Mr. Forsythe has agreed to give Miss Wilder five thousand dollars above the amount for the swimming pool."

"Sporting of him," declared Beverly.

"He must be Santa Claus in disguise," agreed Lenora admiringly. "By the way, what does the star think of the recovery of the films?"

"By 'the star,' I take it you mean Shirley?" Lois asked.

"No other!" declared Lenora.

"Nobody knows what she thinks," Lois answered bluntly. "She keeps to herself most of the time now."

"What a shame," murmured Lenora unfeelingly. "Is it by choice or necessity?"

"Both," Lois answered. "She seems to enjoy being alone. Then, too, none of the seniors will have anything to do with her. The lower classmen, of course, think she is wonderful because she is in the movies. Practically all the freshmen have a crush on her."

"I wonder if we could do something to make her see how foolish she is," murmured Beverly thoughtfully.

"She doesn't speak to me," said Lois loftily, "and I'm quite content."

"It's foolish," Beverly laughed. "Both of you going about like children who have quarreled over a broken doll."

"She started it," Lois said indignantly. "Why should I do anything about it?"

"Your college days are almost over," Beverly said

slowly. "Do you want to remember your senior year because of a quarrel?"

"Stop!" Lenora said grievedly. "I won't be reminded how close we are to commencement. I always feel like crying."

"We won't let that happen," Lois declared promptly. "Suppose we go down to Weller's?"

"Run along," Beverly urged. "I've got some work to do, and you are both distracting elements."

"You don't appreciate us," wailed Lenora. "We go—but we shall return!" she added darkly. "And when we do——"

"Bring me some candy from Weller's," said Beverly practically.

"Righto," surprisingly agreed Lois as the two went out.

CHAPTER XIV

Kidnaped

THE DAYS passed, and with them the winter turned to spring. Leaves began budding on the trees, birds appeared winging their way back from the warm South, bulbs awakened and sprouted their green tips above the brown earth. In everything there was present the spirit of a new life.

The Forsythe Film Company had finished their picture and gone back to Hollywood. Before they went, however, they gave a preview showing of the picture they had made. Every girl who could crowded into the tiny Vernon theater to see it. The story was excellent, speaking well for Beverly's ability as a scenario writer. The actors portrayed their parts marvelously, and the audience was enthusiastic to the point of hilarity. The spectators demanded the presence of Shirley and Conway Grant on the stage. The two bowed to one another and then to the audience. They were overwhelmed with applause. It was no wonder at all if Shirley's head was turned that night.

After the departure of the film company Shirley found herself with a lot of free time on her hands, but she did not use it to renew old friendships. She kept to herself and spent a good deal of her leisure in the library or walking in the woods back of the college.

Beverly was busy with class affairs and scarcely noticed Shirley's inactivity. She had become used to silence in the room she and Shirley shared, and there was no reason for her to seek Shirley out at any other time. The other girls, too, were busy crowding all the pleasures they could into these last weeks of college life.

One afternoon in late April Lenora and Connie Elwood were leaving Weller's when they passed Shirley on the street. Neither of the three spoke, but passed with averted glance and heads high. At the corner Lenora stopped and almost guiltily looked back over her shoulder at the retreating red-headed girl.

"What's the matter?" Connie wanted to know.

"I—I don't know," Lenora said uncomfortably. "I feel as if I should have spoken to Shirley."

"What in the world——" began Connie wonderingly.

"Strange, isn't it?" Lenora laughed. "My feeling

like that. I've never given a hang what she did before."

"To tell the truth," Connie said as the two girls slowly continued on their way, "I've felt rather sorry for her lately."

"The worm has turned," Lenora said lightly. "We are both getting kind hearted."

"She and Beverly haven't made up yet, have they?" Connie asked.

"Shirley has spoken to none of us," Lenora said. "It is a shame, too, in our last year."

The girl they had just passed was thinking the same thing. During the last few weeks she had changed; she knew it but the others did not. The transformation had begun during the Christmas holidays. Little by little she began to realize how foolish she had been in cutting off her friends. She realized how despicable she must have seemed to them. Now she could well understand Lois' attitude when she had declared her, Shirley, "high-hat." She had let Mr. Forsythe and Conway Grant turn her head like a silly schoolgirl. She had let a little taste of popularity and success take possession of her until all she could see was her own importance.

She had spent some lonely hours during the Christmas holidays, and she had had plenty of time to think. Her thoughts had not been pleasant. More than once she had had her hand on the telephone to make a long-distance call to Beverly to apologize for the way she had acted. Always something interfered between her and her intention. Perhaps it was pride that held her back. She wished now she had gone ahead impulsively and called Beverly. The blue-eyed girl would have understood. Beverly seemed always to understand her better than any of the other girls. When Shirley had returned to Vernon she had been prepared to become friends with Beverly, but she really had had no chance, she told herself. Beverly was busy, and when she had a few minutes' spare time she sought out the company of Anne or Lois or Lenora. Of course, Shirley should have expected that. Beverly was no mind reader: she could not tell that Shirley was different now than when she had left for her vacation.

The production on the picture had gone forward, and Shirley had worked faithfully, doing her part. Day after day she had worked with Lois, and each time she had encountered Lois' gaze she had flushed uncomfortably. Once she and Lois had been good friends, and now Lois despised her. Well, what had she expected after the way she had behaved?

Even on the night of the preview of her picture, when the girls had applauded her enthusiastically, she had responded smilingly, but she felt as though she wanted to run away and hide some place. She had received the congratulations and praises with a heavy heart. Truly success could be empty if one lost friendships because of it. She would never forgive herself for refusing to play in that basketball game. She had let down all her friends and cost the seniors the championship of the school. As a result the girls ignored her, and she could not blame them. How could she have been so stuck-up as to refuse when Beverly asked her to play? After all, she had only spent a miserable evening watching the seniors' defeat.

Other times, when she was away from senior activities, she had gone to the movies with Conway Grant only to please her own vanity. Other girls might have been thrilled to sit in a darkened theater beside the movie star, but Shirley had been bored. She had been thrilled when Conway Grant asked her to the theater, and she had accepted with pleasure, but he had not been as entertaining as she had expected, and she really regretted having gone with him. How much better it would have been if she had not starred in the picture at all! Perhaps she would not have lost all her friends then.

She sighed and looked about her. Almost unconsciously she had walked along until she found herself on the outskirts of the town. Reluctantly she turned and headed back to the college. It would soon be dinner time. But she hated to go back. Every time she faced Beverly she felt like kicking herself. She longed to break down the reserve that had grown up between them, but she could not. In this, her last term of college life, she wanted to be the best of friends with all the Alphas once more, but she could find no way to bring that about. If she went openly and apologized to them, it might do no good. They might accept her apology kindly and go no farther than that. She wanted really to be friends again, not merely acquaintances. If they wouldn't, after she had made the attempt, it would hurt her deeply. She was afraid to try. If they did refuse to go back to the old terms she wouldn't know what to do. Now things were undecided, but at least she had hopes that some day she would be accepted again into the old Alpha group.

She wondered if Connie and her friends had been elected members yet. She had been utterly foolish in being so opposed to Connie. Lately she had heard some rather nice things about Connie. The girl was really worth knowing, and yet she had given that foolish ultimatum of resignation if Connie was accepted as an Alpha member. Oh, she, Shirley, had done some foolish things this term, and she heartily regretted each and every one of them. If there was only something she could do——

A machine had pulled up shortly in front of

her. Two men got out and stood as though waiting for her to come up to them. The road, at this point, was deserted, and she felt a momentary thrill of fear. Then she sternly reproved herself. They probably only wanted to ask directions. Possibly they were lost and she could put them right. She continued on at her leisurely pace. When she reached them, one of the men beckoned to her. She had been right: they wanted to ask directions.

When she came near enough, one man grabbed her and the other opened the car door. Shirley screamed, but a rough hand closed over her mouth. She kicked and fought and succeeded in loosening the hold of the man. But in a moment the other man had seized her and was pushing her into the automobile. Shirley was strong and agile, but she could not compete with the two men. They completely overpowered her, and the machine drove off with Shirley a prisoner.

CHAPTER XV

Ransom Note

BEVERLY opened the door to her room and looked about. The room was in complete darkness, and when she lighted the desk light there was a frown on her face. The room was empty. Shirley was not here, and she had not been to dinner. Beverly could find no explanation for the girl's absence. Even when she had been busy with work on the picture, Shirley had always come to Chadwick Hall for her meals. She could not understand where the girl might be tonight. Now there was nothing to keep her away from the Hall, why had she not come for dinner? She had not seen Shirley since lunch time. Lenora had said she and Connie Elwood saw Shirley on Main Street late in the afternoon, but since then no word had been heard from her.

Beverly took a book and settled down to read for a while. Only the ticking of the clock on the desk and the occasional turning of pages disturbed the stillness of the room. Study hour came and went, and the lights-out bell rang. Noiselessly Beverly put out her light and slipped into pajamas and dressing gown. Then she cautiously opened her door and peeped out. Across the hall Lois and Anne, too, peeped out. The three exchanged nods and slipped from their rooms. Silently they headed for the stairs. Today was Rosalie's birthday, and Lenora was holding a fudge party for her. Every one of their friends was invited.

Mrs. Dennis had gone out tonight, and Beverly was in sole charge of the Hall. She had had some misgivings as to whether it was right to attend the party or not when she was supposed to enforce rules and parties were taboo. But it was several weeks since she had attended one, and tonight was a special occasion, so she threw her conscience to the winds and decided to go. She was tired of studies and class work. She was determined to have a good time tonight, even if Mrs. Dennis discovered the merrymakers and she had to resign from her position in the Hall.

Beverly, Anne, and Lois crept up the stairs to the next floor and knocked at Lenora's door. It was opened noiselessly, and they were ushered in.

"You're early," Rosalie greeted them.

"So you can help make the fudge and chocolate and sandwiches," said Lenora practically.

"I think I'll go out and come back later," Lois said. "I don't feel like working."

"You will help or you don't get anything to eat," announced Lenora.

"In that case, I'll help," Lois said resignedly.

All the cushions that could be were borrowed, and as the guests arrived they dropped down on them. There were the Alpha members, minus Shirley, and Connie and her friends. All the girls were clad in comfortable pajamas and dressing gowns. Evelyn DeLong had brought along her ukulele, and as they munched their refreshments the girls hummed the latest songs. The laughter and singing kept up until late into the night, until every scrap of the lunch the girls had prepared was gone. Everyone declared that Rosalie's party had been a huge success when at last they trailed away to their own quarters.

It was long after midnight when Beverly entered her room. A cautious glance showed her that Shirley was not in bed. A worried frown appeared between her brows. Where in the world was Shirley at such an hour? She flung wide the window, and a breeze wet with rain drifted in to her. The sky was clouded over, and the stars and moon had disappeared. Shadows were thick on the campus.

Slowly Beverly turned and crept into bed. Her mind was busy seeking an excuse for Shirley's absence when something came hurtling through the window. It landed on the carpet with a thud. Regardless of regulations, Beverly switched on the light. On the floor lay a stone with a piece of paper tied to it. Mystified, she picked it up and pulled the paper off. With knitted brows she deciphered the almost unintelligible writing. In a minute she had snapped off the light and was back at the window, her eyes seeking the outline of a figure on the ground below. But the shadows were too thick. She could see nothing. In another second she was slipping into a dressing gown and running up to Lenora's room.

She knocked at the door, and Lenora drowsily opened it.

"Go back to bed," Lenora implored with a yawn. "The party is over."

"I'm not here for a party," Beverly said grimly. She entered the room and closed the door.

"Hey, what's the idea?" Lenora demanded as Beverly switched on the light. "Do you want the Dean down on our necks?"

"Read that!" Beverly thrust into Lenora's hands the note that had come hurtling through her window.

"It's too much like a puzzle for so late at night," Lenora said, sinking down on the bed.

"Read it!" Beverly insisted, pacing back and forth.

Something of Beverly's agitation crept into the minds of Rosalie and Lenora, and the two bent over the crude note.

"Where did this come from?" Rosalie asked in amazement.

"It was thrown through my window," Beverly answered. "Do you understand what it means?"

"Of course," Lenora said dazedly. "Shirley has been kidnaped, and the kidnapers demand ten thousand dollars from her parents."

"What shall we do?" Beverly cried.

"What is there to do?" Rosalie asked. "Her parents will have to pay the sum."

"The kidnapers say that Beverly should place the money in a hollow stump thirty paces to the east of the old Horler Mansion the day after tomorrow," continued Lenora consulting the paper in her hand.

"And also that she should not notify the police," added Rosalie.

"I'll telephone her parents first thing in the morning," Beverly said. "I'll also go to Miss Wilder. Will you come with me, Lenora?"

"Of course," Lenora said promptly. "I wouldn't miss it for the world. Gosh, something is always happening to one of the Alphas, isn't it? Last year

Beverly was kidnaped by the gypsies, and now——"

"This is a whole lot more serious," Beverly said frowning. "It is deadly serious. They might—kill her!"

"Not when they have a chance of getting a fortune in money," said Lenora bluntly.

"Why do you suppose they picked on Shirley?" Rosalie murmured.

"She is in the movies, and her father is a millionaire," explained Lenora patiently. "They have more chance of getting a large sum of money from her people."

"This is terrible," groaned Beverly, still restlessly pacing. "I'm worried sick."

"I guess we all are," admitted Lenora. "After all, Shirley was a great girl."

Beverly laughed shakily. "We find that out now. What good does it do?"

Lenora caught hold of her friend's arm. "Sit down, Bev. Don't be so worried. After all, money will free her."

"But will her parents pay the ransom?" Beverly asked. "They might prefer to fight."

"You have to talk them out of it," Lenora declared. "The kidnapers have made you the go-between, and you have to see that their orders are carried out or——"

"Or else——" echoed Beverly significantly. "Lenora, we have to do something!"

"Play detective again," said Lenora thoughtfully.

"We have to keep this news of kidnaping quiet," Beverly continued slowly. "We will circulate the word that Shirley is confined to her room with a cold. Day after tomorrow you and I will go out to the Horler Mansion and place the money."

"What if the kidnapers don't keep their word?" Rosalie cut in.

"We might be able to think of a way to outwit them," Beverly said, running her fingers through her hair nervously.

"That is doubtful," said Lenora. "They will be on the lookout for any tricks."

"Just the same," Beverly said slowly, "we might think of something."

"Whatever it is, count me in on it," declared Lenora. "And now what are we going to do—go back to bed?"

"I suppose so," Beverly said frowning. "There is just one thing, if we should be able to do something for Shirley, we won't let her know who did it."

"What do you mean? She is bound to know," Lenora replied.

"We will tell her the authorities did everything,"

said Beverly. "Once before she became great friends with us through—gratitude."

"I understand," Lenora nodded. "Whatever we do it is merely in the interests of justice, not because of her. If she thought we helped her in any way, she might become friends because she felt she had to. We will be as discreet as clams."

"Another thing, only us three and Mrs. Dennis and of course Miss Wilder are to know of it," added Beverly.

"We understand," nodded Lenora and Rosalie.

Beverly went back to her room and to bed, but not for a long while to sleep. She lay awake in the darkness staring up at the ceiling. Shirley had been kidnaped, and the kidnapers demanded ten thousand dollars for her safe return. Shirley had been kidnaped! That thought went round and round in her mind. Suppose Shirley's parents refused to pay the ransom? Suppose Shirley was not safely returned? A hundred possibilities came uppermost to terrify her.

One thing was certain: she would do anything in her power to help Shirley, but Shirley must never know. Once before they had become great friends because Shirley felt grateful for what Beverly had done. In their freshman year Beverly had rescued Shirley from the Hall fire, and immediately the red-headed girl had apologized for her past behavior, and they had started as friends. But now Beverly wanted Shirley to become friends not through gratitude for anything that she, Beverly, might do, but because Shirley sincerely wished to be friends. Beverly wanted nothing to influence Shirley. The other girl should go her way unbiased by Beverly's actions, and when Shirley had had enough of this estrangement she would make the first overture of friendship.

After a while Beverly fell into a troubled sleep, but it was to dream frightful dreams in which she and Lenora and Shirley were all fighting off unknown demons.

CHAPTER XVI

Rescue

It was raining lightly when Lenora and Beverly started out. They wore heavy raincoats and berets, pulled down rakishly. Beverly carried a square parcel done up in brown paper. It was a precious package—containing the asked-for ransom.

"It would have to rain," grumbled Lenora as they sloshed along College Avenue. "I hope we don't have to stay out very long."

"We are going to stay out and try to catch a glimpse of these—kidnapers," said Beverly determinedly.

"It's a good thing her father brought that money this morning," Lenora commented briefly. "It seems a foolish thing to do, though, to put that sum in a hollow tree stump."

"We've got to take the chance, haven't we?" Beverly demanded. "I had a hard time talking her father out of coming with us."

"You are supposed to be coming alone," said Lenora.

"I don't want to carry all this money by myself," declared Beverly. "I don't see why they picked on me as the one to act for them. I don't like it."

"Where is your sense of adventure?" jeered Lenora. "This is exciting."

"So you think," returned Beverly. "Well, there is the old mansion."

"Now to measure off thirty paces to the east," said Lenora.

The two began pacing off the distance and came upon a broken-off tree stump.

"Are we on time?" Lenora asked. "Remember, the note said four-thirty."

"It is exactly four-thirty," Beverly answered, consulting her wrist watch. "And nobody is in sight."

"Did you expect them to shake hands with you?" demanded Lenora. "Put the money in the stump and come along. I'm ankle deep in mud."

Beverly placed the money in the hollow stump, and the girls turned and made their way back the way they had come. When they came to the Horler Mansion Beverly pulled Lenora into the house.

"What's the idea?" Lenora wailed. "I don't like this dusty place."

"Come along upstairs," Beverly commanded. "From the side bedroom we can see the hollow stump where the money is."

"Ah, then we can see who comes for it," exclaimed Lenora. "Come on, race you up."

The two clattered up the stairs, scattering dust in clouds, and the noise echoing like thunder through the deserted house. They went into the east bedroom and stood at the window.

"You go into the front room and watch the road," proposed Beverly to Lenora. "Tell me the minute you see anyone going along the road."

"Righto," Lenora responded and departed.

At their different posts the two girls watched the road and the hollow stump wherein reposed ten thousand dollars. The minutes ticked away, and nervously Beverly glanced at her watch. It was quarter to five. The kidnapers were fifteen minutes overdue. Did they suspect that they were being watched and would not come out into the open until the two girls went back to the college? The directions that had been printed on the piece of paper had been followed implicitly. Only Lenora and Rosalie and Shirley's parents, together with Mrs. Dennis and Miss Wilder, knew that Shirley was not confined to her room with a heavy cold. Had the note been merely a hoax?

"A car just went up the road," announced Lenora, appearing in the doorway.

"Good!" Beverly motioned her friend to the window. "Stay here and keep your eyes glued to that stump. After the men have taken the money, wait fifteen minutes for me. If I'm not back in that time, go on to the Hall, but don't tell a soul about what I've done."

"But where are you going?" Lenora demanded.

"I'll tell you all about it when I come back," Beverly said, already disappearing into the hall. "Remember—don't breathe a word to anybody!"

Beverly dashed out of the house and through the surrounding trees. Speedily she ran up the road, keeping a sharp lookout for a parked automobile. At last she saw it, drawn off to one side. She waited in the shelter of the trees for some sign of life in the machine, but there was none. She was about opposite the place where the hollow stump was. Evidently the kidnapers had arrived in this machine and gone to collect the money. She crept through the rain and trees until she caught a glimpse of two men bending over the stump where she had placed the money. Then she turned and ran back to the road.

The automobile was a coupé, with a large luggage carrier in the rear. Beverly opened the carrier and peered in. It was empty, and in a second she was inside. They were rather cramped quarters, but she was determined to play detective and track the desperadoes to their lair, as the detective stories put it. It was dark and stuffy in here, but she would have to stand it until the kidnapers got under way.

She heard the men tramp up to the automobile and get in. For one wild minute she thought they were going to open the luggage carrier, but they did not. With a roar the engine started, and the car backed bumpily onto the road. As it shot forward in response to the driver's urgent pressure, Beverly lifted the cover of her hiding place a few inches. The air that seeped in was cool and wet with rain. At every bump they went over Beverly gritted her teeth. Tomorrow she would be full of bruises. This certainly wasn't a comfortable way to ride.

She had been foolish to climb in here. She had no idea where the men were going, and yet she was going too. She had acted on impulse, and she now began to realize how foolhardy she had been. The men might, as she had hoped, take her to Shirley, but how could she hope to free her friend? Every minute they were getting farther and farther away from Vernon and any assistance that Beverly might need. She should have just left the money and returned to Vernon as the note had instructed. Tomorrow Shirley might have been returned unharmed. Ah, yes, might have been! That was what had made her act as she had. How did she or the others know that the kidnapers would keep their word? Having once gotten ten thousand dollars, they might demand a much larger sum and still hold Shirley a prisoner.

An exclamation escaped her as the machine bounced over a deeper rut. It was very uncomfortable back here. She hoped that they didn't have much farther to go. She would be in pieces after a few more shakings. The voices of the men in front drifted back to her like a dull drone above the patter of the rain. She could distinguish nothing intelligible from their conversation, but they seemed to be in high spirits.

She wished she could peep out and catch a glimpse of the direction they were taking, but she was afraid of discovery. She didn't crave exposure at this stage of the game. If the men found her now she might have to walk back to Vernon. Or, what would be more revolting, they might kidnap her also. She would rather remain a willing stowaway than a captive. While they weren't aware of her presence, she might have a chance to determine their identity and help Shirley. She had not wanted

Shirley to know she, Beverly, had done anything to aid her, but now Shirley was bound to know.

The car went on and on for hours. Twilight settled down over the world. The rain continued in an uninterrupted pour. Beverly's muscles were stiff and cramped from her crouched position, and she was beginning to feel the need of a good warm dinner. Surely they weren't going to drive much farther! They must have come at least fifty miles from Vernon by now.

When at last the car drew to a noisy halt and the men jumped out, Beverly forced herself to remain perfectly quiet. Now that they had reached the end of their journey it would never do for her to be discovered. She heard them walk away and the slamming of what was no doubt the door to a house. She crouched still in the darkness of the luggage carrier, waiting until she could be sure the men were not returning.

Cautiously, after several minutes had passed, she lifted the cover of her hiding place and climbed out. She was stiff all over from her cramped position. She rubbed her muscles as she took in her surroundings.

The car had been driven into a driveway off the road and could scarcely be seen in the darkness. A house, three stories, loomed up out of the shadows, but no light gleamed from any of the windows.

Shades were drawn tight to shut out prying eyes. Across the way a street lamp sent out its sickly yellow glow.

Beverly shivered uncomfortably and turned her coat collar up as protection against the rain. This was a perfect scene for a crime—old house, full of thieves and kidnapers, far away from any other habitation—what a setting for a murder! She rebuked herself. What made her think of those things?

She knew better than to try to gain entrance to the house through the front and splashed around to the back door. An outside shed was built against the house and, lucky for her, the door was unbolted. As noiselessly as a shadow she stepped in and closed the door behind her. She stood for several minutes holding her breath until her eyes became accustomed to the darkness and she could see into what she had let herself. The kitchen was ahead of her, and she went forward slowly. In the darkness she brushed against an aluminum pan on the table, and it clattered to the floor. It sounded like an explosion and sent Beverly scurrying back to the protection of the shed.

A man rushed into the kitchen flashing a light before him. The noise had brought one of the kidnapers to investigate, and Beverly's heart sank. She was bound to be discovered now.

A weak, wavering "Meow" came to both the hidden girl and the man. The latter's flashlight fastened on a cat curled up boldly in the center of the kitchen table.

"Only a cat," the man grunted and swung about and left the kitchen.

Beverly leaned weakly against the wall. What a narrow escape! If it hadn't been for that cat the man would have come into the shed and straight to her. Beverly tiptoed into the kitchen and petted the warm fluffy coat of the kitten. From now on she was the friend of every cat in the world.

The kitchen opened onto the hall, and it was to this door that Beverly went. The man who investigated the crash in the kitchen had come from the room on the right of the hall. That explained to her where the men were gathered. The hall was in darkness, and for this Beverly was thankful. It afforded protection for her. She tiptoed to the door of the room in which the men were and pressed her ear against the panel.

"Have you any more movie stars you want us to kidnap?" a voice demanded jovially. "We've never made ten thousand dollars so easy."

"This is only the beginnin'," another voice interrupted. "Tomorrow you will deliver another note demanding twenty-five thousand."

It was as she had expected! They did not pro-

pose to free Shirley. They would keep on demanding more and more money. They couldn't even
keep the bargain they had made. Beverly stood
undecided, frowning into the darkness. Where was
Shirley? Was she in the room with the others, or
had they locked her in a room by herself? The only
way to find out was to search the house, but that
was risky. If she upset any more pans or made
such a noise again she might not escape as easily
the next time.

As she crossed and entered the room on the other
side of the hall her foot brushed against something
on the floor. She stooped and picked it up. A flashlight! This was luck. She pressed the button and a
round circle of light shot out before her. This room
was the dining room, and deserted save for the
furniture which stood about like shrouded ghosts.
There were steps leading up to the second floor,
and Beverly went toward these. Warily she
mounted them, fearing every minute lest one of
the men should come out of that room and see her.
The steps creaked beneath her weight, and her
heart was in her mouth. If she should be discovered now!

On the second floor three doors confronted her.
All of them were closed. If she entered those rooms,
would she walk right into a trap, or were those
men downstairs the only ones in the building? She

would have to take that chance. She had to reach Shirley, and soon!

Cautiously she opened one door. Only silence greeted her. She flashed her light inquisitively around. The room was empty. The next room and the next were as fruitless. She turned back to the stairs and mounted to the third floor. Shirley must be up here! She boldly flashed her light before her, and it rested on a closed door. A key was in the lock, and she turned it, at the same time putting out her light. She threw the door open and paused on the threshold. The room was in total darkness, but she had heard a movement of some kind. She was immediately on her guard and ready to flee at the slightest indication of danger. She did not propose to be made a prisoner now. Again came that slight movement of another's presence, and then a voice.

"Who is it? What do you want?" the voice was loud, but it trembled despite the forced bravado.

"Shshsh," Beverly cautioned. "Shirley! Are you all right?"

In a moment Shirley had grasped her friend's arm tightly. "Beverly! Is it really you? How did you get here? Don't you know those men are desperate? You should never have come!" she wailed nervously.

"Shshsh, don't talk now," Beverly warned her.

She grasped Shirley by the hand and pulled her along to the door. "We have to go down the stairs and right past the room where they are. Now, don't make any noise or we will be caught!"

"I won't," Shirley promised faithfully. "Only—do you think we can make it?"

"Of course we can," Beverly said confidently. "But—they have ten thousand dollars of your father's money."

"Let them have it!" Shirley said heartily. "Only let us get out of here!"

"We'll try," Beverly assured her. "Steady, now—and not a sound!"

As noiseless as two shadows the girls descended to the second floor and from thence to the first. At the bottom of the long flight of stairs they paused to draw a long breath—but too soon. The door across the hall opened, and a man came out. Beverly drew Shirley into the enveloping folds of a tapestry, and they stood hidden until the man had mounted the stairs out of sight. Then they crept forward to the kitchen. As they reached the outside shed they heard the man upstairs let out a shout.

"He has discovered your escape," whispered Beverly. "Make a run for the car. It's now or never."

The two dashed out into the rain to the automobile. Beverly flung herself into the driver's seat just as a man dashed out after them.

"Lucky I learned to drive a car summer before last," she declared as she started the motor.

"They are almost up to us," Shirley whispered frantically. "Can you start it?"

"Of course I can," Beverly said, and the car leapt ahead in response to her touch.

Beverly turned the car out on the road and threw a glance back at the men they had escaped.

"They're dancing like wild Indians," Shirley laughed.

"I wonder if they have a car to follow us?" Beverly mused. "We will make all the time we can while we can."

Beverly drove the car forward at breath-taking speed. It skidded perilously on the wet roads.

"Do you have to go so fast?" gasped Shirley.

"We'd better," Beverly said. "The men might get a car and follow. We want to get as far away as possible."

Neither girl would soon forget that ride. Beverly drove fast, but what was more dangerous than the speed was the slippery road. The car rocked and swung from side to side like a boat tossed about on a stormy sea. Their only guides to the right roads to take were the signposts at intersections, and Beverly had to slow down whenever they came to one.

"We got away easily, didn't we?" Shirley murmured.

"Almost too easily," Beverly agreed. "I don't like it. I have a premonition that something else will happen yet."

"But what can?" Shirley asked. "We are far away from them now."

"I don't know," Beverly said slowly. "But I didn't think they would let us go so easily."

"They have ten thousand dollars," Shirley commented. "Perhaps they think that is enough."

"Perhaps," Beverly agreed and lapsed into silence. She didn't feel easy about their escape. Surely the men would have followed them or tried in some way to stop them. Why had they permitted the two to escape without any interference? Of course, they might not have had another car with which to follow. That seemed the only explanation, and she adopted it.

Beverly   182

CHAPTER XVII

Arrested

SHE KEPT the car going forward at a rapid pace, and they were coming closer and closer to Vernon, when suddenly disaster fell upon them. A shrill police whistle split the air behind them, and the girls exchanged alarmed glances. Beverly pulled the car to a halt. They were passing through a little suburban town, and Beverly was afraid she had unknowingly violated some traffic rule.

The policeman stalked up to the car, a thunderous cloud on his face.

"Let's see your license," he bellowed.

"I haven't any," Beverly confessed, her heart sinking. What could the authorities do to her for driving without a license?

"Oh," the policeman continued, "driving a stolen car without a license. And you only a slip of a girl!"

"A stolen car?" Beverly echoed.

"That's what I said," he shouted at her. "I'll have to take you to the station house."

"But we didn't steal the car," Shirley cut in.

"Don't try to tell me lies," the policeman said, stepping to the running board. "The station house received a call about an hour ago to be on the look-out for this car and you two girls. Your father told us you took the car and were running away."

"Our father—took the car—running away ——" the girls gasped in amazement.

"Come on, start the car. You have to go to the station house," he directed.

"B-but——" Beverly began.

"Get going," he said with a frown.

It was useless to argue, so obediently Beverly drove to the police station. The chief of police was a stern-faced individual, and the girls realized that they would have a hard time making him believe their fantastic story. Beverly explained about Shirley's kidnaping and everything that had happened up to the time the policeman arrested them.

"I know it sounds fantastic," she said smiling, "but——"

"You will have to think up a better story than that," the chief said gruffly. "Your father said he would come for you, and we are to hold you until he gets here."

"But he isn't our father!" Beverly said vigorously. "I tell you——"

"You will stay right here until he arrives," the chief said sternly. "Then we will hear what he has to say."

"Couldn't we tell him to call Miss Wilder?" Shirley whispered. "Does she know about it?"

Beverly told her how Lenora and she had told only Mrs. Dennis and Miss Wilder, according to the instructions in the note.

"But if we call the school, it will mean a lot of publicity for it, and the Dean wouldn't like that," she sighed.

"But what can we do?" Shirley asked. "We can't let that man pretend to be our father and take us away from here."

"We have to think of something," Beverly agreed. "I didn't think policemen could be as unintelligent as this man is. I don't think he would believe his own brother."

"I've an idea," Shirley said suddenly.

She left the bench on which she and Beverly had been sitting and approached the captain. Beverly watched them with wondering eyes. She hoped Shirley had an idea how to get out of this predicament. She had never dreamed that those men might report the automobile as stolen and that they would wind up in a police court! It had seemed the natural thing to take the car and escape the kidnapers. But now there was a doubt about their escape. If the man appeared and claimed them as his daughters—— The police captain would not believe their story, and there seemed no chance of convincing him.

Shirley returned and slumped down beside Beverly.

"What's the matter?" Beverly asked, smiling. "You look—squelched."

"I am," Shirley retorted. "I told him to call my father in New York, and he said he didn't propose to put in such a long-distance call when it would probably be a fake."

"It is a good thing he didn't," Beverly declared. "Because your father is in Vernon. He brought the ten thousand dollars this morning. I wonder if he would let me call Vernon?" she mused. "I'll have a try at him," she said, grinning cheerfully. "He can do no more than say no."

With anxious eyes Shirley watched as her friend warily approached the police captain. She could see that Beverly was arguing with the captain, and she sighed. It seemed impossible to convince the man of anything. If only the kidnapers did not arrive for hours yet. It was more comfortable here in the police station, and much safer than that old house. And there was always the remote possibility of convincing the captain that the man who had telephoned him was, after all, not their father. It was a brilliant play on the kidnaper's part to have thought of having them arrested! It seemed like a chapter of a detective story. The villains of the play had gotten the police, unwittingly, it was true, to aid them in their plot.

Beverly had, somehow, convinced the captain that it was important that she should call Vernon, and as she picked up the receiver she winked triumphantly at Shirley. Shirley waited, nerves on edge, until Beverly had finished her call and returned to the bench beside her.

"However did you do it?" she demanded. "Did you call my father?"

"Yes, and the captain spoke to him, too."

"I saw that he did," Shirley nodded. "What did Father say?"

"He told the captain to hang on to us until he arrived or the captain would lose his job."

"Dad is a fast worker, at least," Shirley beamed. "If both he and the kidnapers arrive at the same time there will be fireworks."

"Anything for excitement," returned Beverly with a smile. "It will take your father at least a half hour to get here."

The girls kept their eyes glued to the wall clock as the minutes sped away. The scratch, scratch of the captain's pen as he wrote busily was the only sound in the room. They began to grow warm and sleepy.

"Gosh," Shirley stifled a yawn, "if somebody doesn't arrive soon I'll fall asleep."

"Help yourself," Beverly invited. "Your father is overdue now. Good-night!" she said suddenly, tensely.

"What's the matter?" Shirley asked drowsily. "See a ghost?"

"Look! Your father didn't arrive first after all."

"The kidnapers," Shirley whispered excitedly. "What do you suppose they will do?"

"It isn't a question of what they will do," Beverly answered. "It is a question of what the captain will do. If he values his job he will not let them take us out of here until your dad arrives."

Two men entered, and as they approached the captain's desk they smiled with satisfaction at their own cleverness. The two girls they had come after were ready, and now it would be only a few minutes until they would be on their way back to their hideout. Then tomorrow they could demand ransom for two who promised to be worth much.

The men swaggered to the desk and smiled upon the captain. What the two said to the captain the girls could not tell, but that they were not pleased with what the captain said to them was evident.

Their smiles disappeared, and they frowned, talking rapidly while they shot cautious glances about them. There was no other policeman in the room and some of their suspicions subsided. They had thought to walk in here, tell their carefully prepared story to the police, and take the girls back with them. But now something threatened to interfere with their plans. They cast more than one dark glance at the two girls who were watching their every movement.

"I don't like their looks," Beverly murmured. "I hope they don't put up too strong an argument to the captain."

"If only my father would hurry," groaned Shirley. "I'm afraid the captain will make us go with them."

"Uh-oh," Beverly whispered. "One of them is coming toward us."

One man stayed talking to the captain and the other came toward the two girls. He stood squarely before them, his back to the captain of police, and a revolver in his hand.

"You—stand up," he ordered Beverly.

With a quiet smile Beverly stood up. "At your service," she murmured.

"You too," he motioned to Shirley, and she took her stand beside Beverly. "Now, listen. I'm going to have my gun in my hand when we go over there to talk to the captain, and if you don't give him the right answers so we can take you out of here, I'm going to pull the trigger."

"You wouldn't dare," Shirley said quickly. "Committing a kidnaping in a police station!"

"A novel idea, isn't it?" he agreed sarcastically. "I don't suppose it has been done yet. But believe me, I'm not kidding! If you don't help us out it will be just too bad!"

"What do you suppose the captain would be doing while you were pulling the trigger on us?" Beverly asked dryly.

"My partner will take care of him," the man answered. "Come on, walk up to the desk and play your part."

"And if we refuse?" Beverly suggested.

"Then I might as well use the gun now," he said with a smile. "But you are bright girls. You will do as I tell you. It is the best thing."

Shirley and Beverly allowed themselves to be escorted up to the captain's desk by the kidnaper. The man did most of the talking while the girls stood in thoughtful silence.

"Do you at last admit that you were running away from your parents," the captain demanded, "and that these men are friends of yours?" He waited for Beverly's answer.

When she did not answer, she felt the gentle

prod of the muzzle of the gun held by the man behind her. A little chill ran down her back. If she were to blurt out her story of the kidnaping now and accuse these men, would the captain believe her and would this man—shoot? He had been in earnest when he warned them, and she really believed he would do as he said. Shirley threw her a fearful glance. Did she want her, Beverly, to agree with the kidnapers?

Were those footsteps behind her? Evidently not, for the gun still pressed against her.

"Well?" the captain barked. "What's the matter? Why don't you speak?"

Beverly swallowed hard. She had to say something, but——

"Have you forgotten about the telephone call I made?" she asked. "You promised to wait."

"What call did she make?" the one man asked quickly.

"She telephoned to Renville for something or other," the captain answered. "But why does it matter to you? What we are concerned with now is your story. She has told me that you kidnaped this other young lady. If that is so——"

"It was all one of her jokes," the man behind Beverly declared. "Wasn't it?" he asked, the pressure on the gun increasing.

"No," Shirley interrupted. "It wasn't a joke, it was the truth!"

"Why, you——" the one man was beginning when the captain interrupted him.

"Just a minute! If what these girls say is true, you——"

"Of course it isn't true," the man defended. "They have this foolish notion in their heads, and——"

"They can speak for themselves," the captain said. "Well, what have you to say?" he demanded of Beverly.

That annoying pressure was returned to her back. Now the men were excited, and she was inclined to believe that the man would keep his threat to pull the trigger. But then they couldn't return with the kidnapers! If only Shirley's father would come! What could be keeping him? He should have been here a half hour ago. If he had come, they would not now be in this shaky position. Should she tell the truth and see if the man kept his word with regard to the gun? Or should she play safe and speak as the men wanted her to? She glanced from one foreboding face to the other and then to Shirley. Shirley was white and frightened. The captain was glaring at the four of them. He was of the opinion that he was wasting his time. If he only knew how true their story was!

"They want to kidnap us again," Beverly said recklessly. "The story we told you when the policeman brought us here is true. Every word of it! Right now this man is threatening me with a gun!" She heard Shirley gasp and the muttered exclamation of the man behind her. At the same time she threw herself violently to one side. The kidnaper kept his word and pulled the trigger of his revolver, but Beverly was not within range. He had not expected her to lurch suddenly to one side, and the bullet went speeding harmlessly past her.

In another minute an arm had grasped the gun hand of the man, and Beverly and Shirley discovered that the latter's father had entered unheard and unseen by any of them. But the kidnaper was strong, and he shook off the hold of Shirley's father. His companion was holding the police captain at bay with another revolver.

"Stand still, all of you!" the man said breathlessly. He laughed grimly. "In a moment we will be on our way, but before we go it might interest you, captain, to know what these girls told you was the truth. We thought we had a good plan, but we didn't count on their daring, or this fellow," he motioned to Shirley's father. "But we have ten thousand dollars, and that is not bad. Stand still!" he roared as the police captain started forward. "Stand just where you are until we've gone out of that door. If anyone follows us for five minutes, we will send a bullet through him."

Beverly, standing to one side of the group, watched the scene with fascinated eyes. The men's daring was superb. A hold-up in a police station! What irony! Four people and all of them helpless to stop the two men. Her mind caught at a possibility. There was a chance that she——

Cautiously she began to sidle around behind the one man. He was talking to the captain, and his eyes were on him. The attention of both the kidnapers was fastened on the captain, who was positively spluttering with rage. The situation was very injurious to the captain's dignity, and his temper was flaming. How he would have loved to get his hands on the two men before him!

Mr. Parker was standing calmly watching. He realized his helplessness and decided to make the best of it. Shirley's gaze was not on the two men before her, but on Beverly. What was her friend up to?

Beverly had slipped from her pocket the flashlight she had found in the old house earlier in the evening. It was a bit large, but it might serve the purpose. She thrust it against the back of the man before her with a stern command to put up his hands. Her ruse might not have worked if the police captain had not seized that moment of surprise to launch himself at the man who held a revolver under his nose. The force of his attack sent the man staggering backward, and in a moment the captain had possessed himself of the man's revolver.

Meanwhile, Mr. Parker had thrown himself on the other man and was struggling to make him relinquish his hold on the gun. But the man was stubborn and fought savagely for his freedom. He freed himself from Mr. Parker and bounded for the door. On the threshold he ran straight into a policeman. The officer pulled back in surprise, and the man dashed past. The captain had snapped handcuffs on his other prisoner and now turned him over to the speechless policeman and ran out after the escaped man.

Beverly and Shirley were in hot pursuit, and when the captain flung himself into his automobile they entered likewise. Mr. Parker, too, did not propose to be left out of the excitement.

The man who had escaped had jumped into the car Beverly and Shirley had used and was already 'way ahead of them. The captain's car leaped after the other like a flash. Through the streets of the little town they raced, leaving pedestrians staring after them in bewilderment. The rain had stopped, but the streets were not dry, and at each corner they turned the cars skidded alarmingly.

The girls were literally breathless, but they did not propose to miss the excitement of the capture. They crouched down in the tonneau speechless as the car lurched from side to side.

"G-goodness!" Shirley gasped. "D-do you think we will ever catch him?"

"It won't be our fault if we don't," Beverly answered between lurches of the car. "The man is driving like a madman!"

"If he should skid off the road he might be killed!" Shirley continued fearfully.

On through the streets the two machines tore careening from side to side. The rain began again, and splattered the windshield until the driver could scarcely see the road. They turned onto the open highway and streaked away from the town. The spirit of the chase had gripped them all now, and they sat tense as statues while the captain did his best to close the distance between his car and the man he pursued. The night was black around them, and the headlights of the automobiles cut through the dark and driving rain like white blades. Occasionally they passed another car crawling along the road at a snail's pace. They dashed across intersections regardless of traffic and at such times the girls held their breath, expecting any moment that another car would hit them.

The captain might be slow in making his de-

cisions in the station house, but behind the wheel
of his car he was anything but slow. The girls had
thought their ride earlier in the evening was something to remember, but this ride was hair-raising.
The captain had forgotten his passengers entirely
and thought of nothing now but catching the man
ahead of him.

But the man in the car ahead did not propose to
be caught. His freedom depended on this race. His
companion had been caught and was probably already in a cell in the station house. But he was
going to escape his pursuers. The charge of kidnaping combined with that little incident of the
police station was serious, and the captain would
not be lenient with him. He had thrown caution to
the wind and drove with a reckless abandon for
consequences. As he drove he cast anxious eyes over
his shoulder at the car behind. Little by little the
police car was creeping upon him. He pushed the
accelerator farther down, and the little car responded immediately. The wheels spun round on
the road as on polished glass, and the car skidded
halfway round. In a moment he had righted it and
was going forward again, but the delay had cost
him a major part of his lead on his pursuers. The
police car was only a few yards away now, and
creeping forward inch by inch.

"That was a close call," Shirley declared after

the car ahead had skidd 1. "If he does that again we might crash into him."

"At any rate, we will catch him," replied Beverly, her eyes shining with excitement.

"He has given us some chase!" Shirley murmured in awe. "Oh! Did you see him skid that time!"

"We'll all be on our ear at that rate," Beverly declared.

They were approaching another intersection. On each side of the road was a thick growth of trees and it was impossible to see whether anything was coming toward them. The cars continued at their headlong pace, and as the car ahead reached the middle of the intersection disaster bore down on it. A truck loomed up out of the night, coming at a swift rate of speed, and crashed into the kidnaper's car. The little car was completely bowled over. It hovered dangerously on two wheels and crashed over on its top, while the car that was following spun about in a mad effort to avert crashing into the two already wrecked cars. The chase was brought to an abrupt halt when the captain's car slid into a tree.

For a moment the occupants of the latter car were too stunned to fully realize what had happened. Everything had occurred so suddenly as to daze them. The wrecked car was lying on its top, the four wheels sticking grotesquely up into the

air. About it splintered glass lay on the wet road.
The truck, heavy and cumbersome, was scarcely
damaged. The driver was climbing from the seat of
the truck when the captain stiffly crawled from his
own car.

Shirley and Beverly and Mr. Parker, too, clam-
bered from the car to the scene of the wreckage.
Everything was confusion, with the truck driver
and the police captain in hot argument.

"But where is the man who was driving?" Shirley asked in alarm. "Did he get away?"

"He must be under the car," Beverly answered,
and she was right.

Mr. Parker with the captain and the truck driver
succeeded in pulling the man from under the wreck
of his car.

"Oooo!" Shirley squealed. "Is he killed?"

"No," the captain replied dryly. "Far from it.
He will go back with us to the station house none
the worse for wear."

"If we can get the car started," Mr. Parker reminded him. "The way we hit that tree——"

"She'll start," the captain assured him. "It isn't
the first time I've run into a tree."

With the help of the irate driver and his truck
the wreckage of the roadster was pulled to one side
of the crossing, and the truck went on its way. The

captain, his companions, and the now totally sub-
dued kidnaper, climbed back into the police car.
After several futile attempts the engine spluttered
into action, and the captain backed his machine
away from the tree onto the road. In another minute they were on their way back to the station
house. This ride was made at a more leisurely pace
than when they had been in pursuit of the other
car.

It had all happened so quickly that the girls were
still surprised. The man had led them such a swift
chase that it was hardly possible to believe it had
ended so quickly. One minute they had been speeding over the wet roads, and the next they had been
piled up against a tree. And now the kidnaper sat
in their midst, sullen and unresponsive, while they
took him back to jail.

It had been a most exciting evening. Beverly
looked out at the fleeting landscape while she re-
viewed it in her mind. Lenora would be amazed.
How she would have enjoyed the thrilling suspense
and the chase! She had never thought when she left
Lenora that afternoon and climbed into the luggage carrier of that car that she was on the road
to such adventures.

When the car slowed down in front of the station house the two girls climbed from the police

car into the one that had brought Mr. Parker to
the scene. They waited while Shirley's father went
into the station with the captain, and when he reappeared they started back to Vernon. The two
girls had the tonneau to themselves, and they curled
up comfortably. Despite the excitement, they were
both a little sleepy, and the smooth purring of the
car as it traversed the miles did not keep them
awake.

Only when the car bumped to a stop outside the
college gates did Beverly realize that at last they
were back at Vernon. The two left the car and ran
to the Hall through the pouring rain.

Contrary to Beverly's wishes, Lenora had told
Miss Wilder and Mrs. Dennis about Beverly's pursuit of the kidnapers, and the two were anxiously
awaiting her return. When the two girls had explained their exciting adventures they went up to
their room.

The room was in darkness, and as Beverly went
toward her desk to light the lamp she stumbled
wildly over something. Immediately a howl split the
air.

"Good gracious," Beverly laughed as the light
revealed Lenora dancing about on one foot. "Why
did you sit in the dark? I nearly went on my nose!"

"Ooooo, you crippled me," Lenora wailed. "Why
don't you look where you are going?"

"How did I know you would be stretched out in the middle of the floor?" demanded Beverly. "I didn't expect you to be here."

"I decided to wait for you, and this is what I get ——" she groaned. "Tell me about your adventures."

"It was thrilling," Beverly declared. "You should have been there! It was the most exciting time I've ever had. Wasn't it exciting, Shirley?"

"It was breath-taking," Shirley replied.

"And I missed it," Lenora murmured sadly. "Oh, dear. I'm never around when anything exciting happens. Why is it?"

"You fall asleep," Beverly teased.

"I do not," Lenora said indignantly. "Sit down and tell me what happened while I do my good deed for the day and make some hot chocolate for you."

"That reminds me," Beverly said. "I didn't have any dinner. You haven't any sandwiches up your sleeve, have you?"

"I've got some little cakes from Weller's," Lenora answered.

"They will do fine," Shirley declared.

While Lenora brought out chocolate and cakes the girls took turns telling of their adventures. First Shirley explained how the men had lured her to their car and driven off with her. Then Beverly took up the tale from the time she left Lenora in the old house to when the policeman had arrested them for having a stolen car. Shirley dramatically described the incident in the police station and the thrilling chase. Lenora had listened with eyes and ears wide open. Now she was literally hanging on each word. Shirley and Beverly told the tale with their best dramatic gestures and thrilled Lenora.

"Oh, dear," she sighed when they had finished. "To think, when you were being shot at and racing about chasing kidnapers, I was calmly eating my dinner."

"We would have changed places with you," Shirley assured her. "I didn't like it at all."

"I did," Beverly declared. "It was thrilling!"

"You can have all that kind of thrills," Shirley yawned.

"I wish I could have some of them," Lenora murmured. "I'm getting rusty from doing nothing exciting. I crave adventures," she said dramatically.

"Next time there is a kidnaping we will let you be the detective," promised Beverly laughingly. "When I get to be a reporter I'll let you help me run down the stories."

"Tish, that isn't exciting enough," complained Lenora. "I crave excitement with a capital E."

"As a reporter you would get it," Beverly declared.

"That's why you want to be one," Lenora murmured. "I see it all now. Beverly has deep and dark designs on solving all the latest murder mysteries."

"She can have 'em all," Shirley sighed. "I want comfort! I don't relish rides such as we had tonight."

"Well," Lenora stood up and stretched luxuriously, "now that you are all safe and sound in your nest once more, methinks I shall run along to my own particular domicile."

"Where is Rosalie? Didn't she want to keep vigil with you?" demanded Beverly.

"She has a slight cold, and I sent her off to bed," Lenora answered. "Lois and Anne were burning up with curiosity as to where you were at dinner time, but you know me—the soul of secrecy. I let them languish in suspense."

Beverly laughed. "For once in your life you were reticence itself," she commended. "I wonder how you did it."

"I was delighted to keep Lois guessing," beamed Lenora. "Well, ta-ta, see you at breakfast."

She toddled off, and the two adventurers tumbled into bed, tired but still a little thrilled at the thought of their evening's excitement.

CHAPTER XVIII

Resignation

THE NEXT DAY Shirley resumed her classes, and none of the other girls suspected anything other than what had been told them. Mr. Parker went back to the city, and the kidnaping incident was almost forgotten.

Shirley, as the days passed, was sunk in depression. After Beverly rescued her she surely expected to become friends again. But Beverly made no attempt to regain their old footing. She was polite, of course, as was Lenora, but neither invited her to rejoin the Alphas. She didn't realize that they were waiting for her to take the first step, and so she went about with low spirits, afraid to offer friendship for fear it would be rejected.

Rumors had reached her to the effect that the officers of the senior class were trying to decide on a valedictorian for commencement. Ever since Beverly had first mentioned the position in the beginning of the term Shirley had cherished a secret desire to be chosen. But now, with Beverly, as president of the class, against her, she did not have much chance. Then, too, she had failed her classmates in the basketball game. They would hardly choose her for such a position on the most important day of their whole four years.

She knelt by the window of her room and looked out on the campus. Beverly was chatting with a group of girls just below. Most of the girls were lower classmen, and Shirley envied the way in which they all looked adoringly at her roommate. Beverly had the knack of immediately destroying any self-consciousness the younger girls might have felt in chatting with the president of the senior class. She might have been one of them, so wholeheartedly did she join in any discussion with them. Once the lower classmen had been just as eager to gain her, Shirley's, favor, and she had snubbed them. The memory hurt now. Why was she always doing something for which she was sorry afterward? Why couldn't she cultivate the graciousness that was so essentially a part of Beverly?

Another girl joined the group below and put a friendly arm about Beverly's waist. Shirley recognized the newcomer as Connie Elwood. Another girl she had treated shamefully. Somehow she seemed to have made a terrible mess of her senior year. There was scarcely a girl out of the hundreds of students that she could call her friend.

A light knock at the door brought her to her feet. "Come!" she called, and Lenora entered, somewhat hesitantly. Shirley smiled, a trifle ruefully. She could well remember the time when Lenora never paused to knock at the door to this room.

"Hello," Lenora said, coming forward uncertainly.

"Hello," Shirley responded, equally uncertain. "Sit down, won't you?" she asked as Lenora paused uncomfortably.

Then Lenora smiled and sank down on one of the beds. "We aren't used to being polite, are we?" she murmured.

"It does seem strange," Shirley admitted smiling. "Did you want to see Beverly?"

"N-no," Lenora admitted. "I—I came to see you. I want to—that is we have decided——"

"What's the matter?" Shirley asked, mystified.

"There is nothing the matter," Lenora answered. "It is just—I'm on the committee that was chosen to decide on the valedictorian for commencement. We—decided to ask you if you would be it."

"If—I—would——" Shirley began slowly. "You didn't think I would refuse, did you?"

"We—weren't sure," Lenora said confusedly. "You see——"

"I see," Shirley said bitterly. "You didn't want to give me the chance to be a total imbecile. I know what you've been thinking," Shirley said hurriedly as Lenora would have interrupted. "I know what all the girls have been thinking, and you are all right. I was the most conceited snob on the campus," Shirley declared with self-condemnation. She turned and stared out the window. "I don't see why you ever agreed to come and even ask me. I don't deserve it."

"But you will be our valedictorian?" Lenora urged softly. "We really want you to."

Tears misted Shirley's eyes, and she kept her back to Lenora. "How could I refuse even if I wanted to?" she asked.

Lenora hesitated and then placed her hands on Shirley's shoulders and turned the red-headed girl about to face her.

"Has the—old Shirley come back to Chadwick Hall?" she asked softly.

"I've kicked the new one out," Shirley said, smiling with difficulty.

Lenora held out her hand, and Shirley slipped hers into it.

"I hope she never comes back," Lenora declared.

"And now—shall we go down to Weller's and celebrate?"

"I have an allowance that is just longing to be spent," Shirley rejoined.

"And we are just the ones to do it," Lenora declared. "Let's go."

Beverly, strolling with Connie Elwood, watched with surprise when Lenora and Shirley left the Hall arm in arm. Lenora flashed her one significant glance that meant Shirley had accepted her proposition. Beverly had expected Shirley to agree to be valedictorian, but she hadn't expected she and Lenora would immediately become so friendly again. Had the mischievous Lenora discovered a way to help Shirley that she, Beverly, had not even guessed existed?

As for Shirley, she was unspeakably happy. She and Lenora gossiped over their ice cream as they had done before any differences arose between them. Their old relationship was fast growing up again, even though they had made their pact of peace only two hours before. When she returned to her room before dinner, she was happier than she had been since the Christmas vacation. She felt that at last she had taken a step back along the old road again. Perhaps even the other girls would in time prove as ready to accept her again as Lenora had.

Several days later, when Shirley was lying on the bed engrossed in reading the latest magazine, Connie Elwood burst unceremoniously into the room.

"Oh, I beg your pardon," she stopped in confusion. "I was looking for Beverly."

"Beverly had some sort of conference with Miss Wilder, and she isn't back yet," Shirley said rising slowly. "Maybe—I can help you."

Connie could not conceal her total surprise at such an offer coming from one of her arch enemies. She decided to overlook Shirley's past snobbishness and explain what was troubling her.

"I don't think you can help," Connie said ruefully, "but I hope somebody can."

"Hullo, what's up?" Lenora broke in upon them. "Hi, Shirley. Greetings, Connie."

Shirley could see that Lenora was puzzled to see her and Connie together—peaceably, and she smiled to herself.

"Connie was looking for Beverly," she explained. "Something is the matter, but I haven't found out what it is yet."

"I'll tell you," Connie interrupted. "Beverly has resigned from the tennis team."

"Beverly—has what?" Lenora shouted, straightening up from her comfortable, if ungraceful, position on a pile of cushions.

"But—if Beverly doesn't play we will lose the championship," Shirley murmured concernedly.

"You are right," Connie declared. "When Wayne postponed the championship match from September to June we thought we were lucky because it would give us time to polish up on our players. Now we are going to lose our star!"

"Does Anne know?" Shirley asked.

"Of course, she must," Lenora cut in. "Anne is captain. Beverly must have submitted her resignation to her."

"She did," Connie said. "It was Anne who told me about it. She tried to talk Beverly out of it, but it was no use."

"Can't we do something about it?" Shirley demanded.

"If Beverly doesn't play we will lose the cup," wailed Lenora. "We've got to do something."

"But what?" Connie asked. "If Beverly doesn't want to play, we can't make her."

"I think she wants to play," Shirley cut in.

"Then why——"

"I don't know." Shirley shook her head. "Hasn't she said anything to one of you?"

"No," Lenora frowned. "Did she tell you about it?"

"No," Shirley admitted, and the color mounted to her cheeks.

Lenora could have bitten her tongue for her thoughtlessness. She had not supposed that Shirley and Beverly were still distant. She thought surely they had forgotten their past difficulties and disagreements.

"Here she comes now," Shirley said, glancing out the window. "She is just entering the Hall."

A few minutes later Beverly was pounced upon by two worried, demanding girls. Shirley would have liked to add her voice to the complaints voiced by Lenora and Connie, but now, as always, she felt the old reserve rising up between them.

"What do you mean by it?" Lenora was demanding.

Beverly smiled. "Just what I said. I'm no longer on the team."

"Did Anne accept the resignation?" asked Connie.

"What else could she do?" Beverly said. "I'm not going to play in the championship match, and that is all there is to it."

"We will lose the cup if you don't," wailed Lenora. "Beverly, please———"

"You will lose if I do play," Beverly declared. "I haven't the time to devote to practice. I couldn't hope to be in fine shape for the match."

"You could easily beat the Wayne players," Lenora insisted.

"Is the fact that you have no time to practice the only reason why you resigned?" Connie demanded.

"That, and—and other reasons," Beverly said uncomfortably.

"Tell us the other reasons," Lenora declaimed. "We will sweep them to one side as insignificant."

Beverly smiled quietly. "Really, girls, I've made up my mind. It took me a long time to decide, but now I know nothing will make me change my decision."

"Beverly, you've just got to," Connie pleaded. "We wouldn't stand a chance if you weren't on our team. Anne was planning to have you and me play together."

"Where is your school spirit?" chimed in Lenora. "You can't resign now when the match is to be three weeks from now."

"Don't make the mistake I made." Shirley spoke for the first time.

The other girls exchanged glances. The situation now was almost the same as it had been when Shirley refused to play in the senior basketball game.

Anne entered at that point and averted an embarrassing silence.

"Oh, Beverly, I came to ask if you won't reconsider about resigning from the tennis team," Anne began.

"We are trying to persuade her to do the same thing," Connie declared.

"It's no use," Beverly said, shaking her head.

"But, Beverly," Lenora groaned, "think of what the other girls will say."

"I won't have time to practice," Beverly insisted. "I wouldn't be——"

"We promise to see that you have time to practice," Lenora cut in.

"We will take over some of your work," Anne agreed. "Come on, Beverly, say you will play."

"We need you on the team," added Connie. "We aren't any good without you."

"B-but," Beverly began, then she smiled resignedly. "All right, I'll take the resignation back. But remember, if I play terribly it is your fault."

"Yyppee!" Lenora tossed the pillows into the air. "Make way for the champions!"

"I'm off to tell Lois," Anne said and departed as suddenly as she had come.

"And I'm going to Weller's," Lenora declared.

"I'll go with you," Connie offered. "How about you, Shirley?"

The other girl came forward smilingly. "I'm willing."

"Beverly?" Lenora paused.

"Nope, I've got to look over bids for the Senior Prom," Beverly declined.

"See you later," Lenora and Connie sang out as the three of them departed.

Beverly stared at the door reflectively. She had never expected to see what she had just seen—Shirley going out with Connie Elwood. Would wonders never cease? First Shirley became friendly with Lenora and now with the girl she had been so opposed to. What was the explanation?

CHAPTER XIX

The Big Game

IT WAS the first of June, the day of the championship tennis match between Vernon College and Wayne Seminary. The visitors from Wayne had descended on the town of Vernon the day before, and the girls of Vernon had provided royal entertainment. The courts of Vernon had been rolled and marked until they were in perfect condition. A grand stand had been erected, and tickets sold rapidly.

Beverly had managed to get in a good deal of practice on the courts between her other activities, and the Vernon team was in better form this year than they had been other terms. Connie and Beverly had been elected to play the final and most important match of the day. The two made a good team, because Connie had a hard, direct manner of hitting, while Beverly was the fastest and lightest on her feet of the Vernon girls.

Anne and Kathleen Ryan were to play the first preliminary match, and two other girls the second preliminary. If the Vernon players emerged triumphant from those two matches, the championship was assuredly theirs. But if they were defeated, then the whole responsibility of winning the cup rested on Beverly and Connie.

The day of the matches was a splendid June day. The sky was a cloudless blue, and the sun was out in full force. For the fans it was an ideal day, but the players found it uncomfortably hot. The grand stand was crowded with exuberant girls, and the Deans of both colleges were seated in a box to watch their respective teams struggle for a silver loving cup.

The referee sat in her high chair, able to command an unobstructed view of the courts. The net was tightened, and Anne and Kathleen and the two Wayne girls took their places for the first game of their set. The spectators were hushed and attentive. The little white ball bounded back and forth between the four players. The score went from deuce to advantage and back again. Anne and Kathleen were good players, but the Wayne girls proved more than a match for them. They went down in defeat to the score of 6-4, 6-5, 6-4.

"Never mind," consoled Lenora as she and Beverly and Connie greeted the players as they came from the court. "We haven't lost the cup yet."

"We've made a wonderful beginning," grumbled Kathleen.

"Maybe our next match will be better," Anne said as she instructed the next two Vernon players.

The two Vernon girls listened to what their captain had to tell them and went on the court determined to win. The Wayne spectators were jubilant over their first easy victory and confidently expected the next to be as successful. But the Vernon girls were determined that this time the score would be in their favor. The Vernon fans gave their players plenty of enthusiastic support. As the ball bounded back and forth, it became evident that the Vernon players were far superior to the Wayne girls, and when the set was over the Vernon girls were triumphant. So it was with the three sets.

"We have a wonderful chance for the cup now," Lenora said rapturously as the girls waited for the time when Connie and Beverly should be called on the court.

"The score is tie, and it all depends on us," groaned Connie. "I hope the Wayne players aren't very good."

"They will be the best players they have," Beverly declared. "We must expect that."

"Then woe is us," murmured Connie sadly.

"What do you mean?" demanded Lenora. "You are the best we have. You have to win that cup for us!"

"We'll try," Beverly promised.

"We'll do our best," Connie added.

"Time to go on," Anne cautioned them.

"Cheerio," Beverly and Connie sang out as they grasped their racquets and approached the net to shake hands with their opponents.

The Vernon spectators gave their players a glorious reception when the two appeared on the court. The Vernon girls knew well the prowess of their star players, and they expected an easy victory.

But the Wayne girls felt equally certain of victory for their players. The Wayne girls were a perfect combination of force and speed. Every time the ball bounded into their court they returned it promptly and with marvelous effect on the score.

The previous preliminary matches had contained three sets each, but now this final and deciding match was played for the best out of five sets. The winners would be presented with the large silver loving cup, and the Vernon girls had their hearts set on it. But then, unfortunately, so had the Wayne girls. The match promised to be most exciting and the most interesting played yet.

Beverly and Connie, for all their combined efforts and agility, went down in defeat at the end of the first set to the score of 6-3. The second set they rallied somewhat and put their opponents to their uttermost, but the Wayne girls proved to be better players than any of the Vernon girls had expected and defeated them.

In the third set Connie and Beverly set their chins determinedly and played tennis as they had never played before. The Wayne girls did their utmost to wrest victory away from the Vernon players, but Connie and Beverly were not to be beaten this time. The score stood in their favor when one of the Wayne girls served a slow net ball. Beverly launched herself forward to catch it on the first bounce. Her foot slipped, and she fell, twisting her ankle under her. The Vernon spectators held their breath until Beverly was on her feet again. If anything happened to their star player now, the game was certainly lost! But Beverly continued to play, and the Vernon girls cheered.

Beverly's lips were set grimly, and her mouth was white about the corners. Connie saw these distress signals and tried to relieve Beverly of as much playing as she could. Something was wrong, and the junior did not stop to find out what it was. This set needed winning, and she was determined they should not lose.

Beverly, as she waited for the Wayne girl to

serve, sent a glance up into the stands. She knew where her friends were sitting. Lenora and Shirley had taken seats together, but now the seats were not occupied. Her eyes came down to the sidelines where Lois and Anne were standing. What she saw there filled her with a glorious happiness. Shirley was shaking hands with Lois! The two who had quarreled so bitterly months before had made up. She was glad. Shirley was slowly regaining her old place in the affections of the seniors. In the past weeks more girls had begun being friendly again with the red-headed girl, and Beverly was thankful.

The Wayne player served a ball that bounded high into the air. Beverly leapt up for it and sent it smashing back far out of reach in the other court. That was the deciding point. At last the Vernon girls had won a set! But what that last point had cost Beverly! She caught hold of Connie's arm to steady herself as they left the court for a seven-minute rest in the locker room.

"What's wrong?" Connie asked anxiously. "You look so——"

"I'll be all right," Beverly gasped. "I just want to lie down for a few minutes."

"Of course," Connie said. "I'll see that no one disturbs you. I wish you would tell me what the matter is," she said worriedly as she helped Beverly into the locker room and the latter sank down thankfully on the wicker divan.

"I'll be all right," Beverly insisted. "You better rest too."

"I'll go outside with the other girls," Connie said. "You lie down and get a grip on yourself. We have two hard sets to play yet."

"I know it," Beverly sighed. "And I don't know how I will get through them," she added to herself as Connie left her.

That last set had been hard. After her fall, it had been sheer pluck that carried her through. She could never do it again.

CHAPTER XX

Victory

BEVERLY lay back and closed her eyes. It was gloriously cool here, and the seven-minute rest granted before the next two sets was all too short. She dreaded the time when she must rise and go forth to the court as though nothing at all were the matter. The door to the locker room opened and closed again, but the silence was not broken.

"Who is it?" Beverly asked wearily, her eyes closed.

"It—is I," Shirley's voice answered her. "Connie said—something was wrong with you. What is it?" She came and stood beside Beverly, looking down at her, gray eyes pleading.

"It is nothing," Beverly insisted. "I was just—played out."

"That isn't like you," Shirley said slowly. "You've often played three straight sets of tennis."

"I saw you shaking hands with Lois," Beverly said directly. "It gave me inspiration for that winning shot."

Shirley smiled and sat down beside her roommate. "Yes. We've agreed to let bygones be forgotten. I didn't suppose she would ever want to speak to me again, but—she does."

"I'm glad you've patched up your quarrel," Beverly said softly.

"I've apologized to everyone but—you," Shirley said slowly. "I've told them all how sorry I am for the way I acted."

"You don't have to apologize to me," Beverly said quickly. "You've done nothing so very terrible."

"I behaved like a tyrant," declared Shirley. "I don't see why the girls put up with me—least of all you. I must have been a terrible roommate while I was working in that movie."

"You threatened to have your room changed and ——" Beverly was beginning.

"And I was scared to death you would take me up on it," Shirley confessed. "I said that when I was angry and afterward I knew I didn't mean a word of it. When I began to realize how shamefully I must have acted I was afraid to apologize for fear you would tell me to take my apology and go jump in a lake. I would have deserved it," she declared.

"And my pride wouldn't let me make up with you," Beverly admitted. "I suppose we both have behaved like silly geese."

"Well, now that we understand one another," Shirley said determinedly, "I want to know what is wrong with you. I know something is, because, as Lenora would say, you look a little green around the gills."

Beverly told herself it was no wonder, but she stoutly insisted that she was as fit as when she had entered the match. Nothing would make her quit the game now. She and Connie had to win this final set and carry off the silver loving cup. The Vernon girls were all rooting for them, and Beverly would not shirk. She knew that the other girls on the Vernon team would not stand a chance against the terrific playing of the Wayne girls. Connie and she were the two strongest players at Vernon, and she was going to do her part to bring off the match triumphantly.

The rest period ended, and the players went back on the court. The spectators were beside themselves with excitement. These last two sets were vitally important. If the Wayne players won one more set the cup would be theirs. The Vernon rooters supported their team with uproarious cheering every

time Connie or Beverly scored a point. The Vernon
players had every one of their schoolmates standing behind them. For that matter, so did the Wayne
girls. The visitors were yelling themselves hoarse,
and the players seemed to have gained a new source
of energy during the seven-minute rest period.
They bombarded the Vernon girls with fast and
furious balls, and Beverly and Connie were hard
put to hold their own.

Beverly's lips were closed tightly, and her eyes
were shadowed with pain, the source of which was
a complete mystery to her friends. Every step she
took was torture to her, and yet she grimly refused
to give up and forfeit the cup to their opponents.
Connie shielded her partner as much as she could,
which was indeed very little. The Wayne girls sent
ball after ball crashing at Beverly, and they were
returned successfully, sometimes not.

When the fourth set was ended the Vernon girls
were triumphant. The score was tied. Each side had
won two sets. The championship depended on this
last set, and the spectators sat as though enthralled.
The Vernon girls looked totally worn out, as
though it would be a physical impossibility to
weather the strain of the next set. Even the Wayne
girls were appearing tired. They had played hard
and fast, never meaning the match to run the full
five sets.

Beverly was serving, and the ball bounded from court to court as the girls fought for the first point. The fans in the grand stand were breathless, hanging on every movement of the players. Every time a point was scored a cheer went up from that respective section. The air was tense with excitement. It was a match that would be remembered always in the schools' tennis history.

Game after game was played, and the score went from deuce to advantage and back again. The four girls fought grimly, relentlessly. Each side was determined to emerge triumphant.

"Oh," Lenora groaned. "What is the matter with Beverly?"

A burst of applause came from the spectators.

"Good for Connie! What a shot!" Lois danced in excitement. "We only need one more point."

The ball left the racquet of the Wayne girl and bounced far forward in the Vernon court. Beverly leaped at it and sent back a slow net ball that barely skimmed the net, bounced once, and rolled to a stop.

It was such an abrupt ending to the match that had been so long and fought so bitterly that the spectators did not at once grasp the fact that it was over. Then, such cheers as rent the air! The Vernon girls were beside themselves with joy and pride.

The silver loving cup was theirs! They were the champions!

"Isn't it simply—scrumptious?" demanded Lenora hugging Lois ecstatically. "Such playing! It was the most exciting match I've ever seen!"

"It was superb, magnificent——" Lois began.

"Colossal!" finished Shirley. "You sound like a —— Look! What's happened?"

"I don't know," Anne answered.

The four started on a run for the court. Beverly and Connie had come forward to shake hands with their vanquished opponents. As they did so, Beverly grasped once at Connie's arm and, with a little sigh, collapsed.

CHAPTER XXI

United

THE GIRLS took her to the locker room, and anxious hands rendered all manner of restoratives, but they weren't necessary.

"What a p-perfectly silly thing to do!" Beverly declared, sitting up dazedly.

"You scared us all half to death," asserted Lenora. "Why ever did you do it?"

"Silly, she didn't want to do it," defended Lois.

"Of course I didn't," Beverly said, "but I wrenched my ankle in the third set, and——"

"And you went on playing!" finished Connie admiringly.

"I didn't want to forfeit the cup," answered Beverly. "I could never do it again, though."

Each one of the girls promptly declared that they would never have done it—cup or no cup. After a few minutes' rest, the girls assisted Beverly out to the court once more, and there the cup wa⸗

presented to the winning couple, amid much cheering and speech-making.

It had been agreed that after study hour the six Alphas and the six girls that hoped to join the group as full-fledged members were to gather in Beverly's and Shirley's room. As soon as the study-hour bell rang through the building, books were slammed shut and pajama-clad figures began to steal silently through the corridors.

"We ought to have a password," declared Shirley as she opened the door to admit Lois and Anne.

"Or a signal knock," agreed Lenora, who, with Rosalie, had been the first to arrive. "It would be terrible if we let in the wrong people."

"Who would want to get in?" Lois demanded lazily. "We are lucky we have as many members as we have."

"Is zat so?" Lenora was beginning indignantly when another knock heralded the arrival of Connie Elwood and Kathleen Ryan.

The two entered bearing mysteriously covered dishes.

"Ah!" Lenora beamed on them. "What have we here?"

"Cream puffs," answered Kathleen. "We raided the kitchen and coaxed them from the cook."

"The only objection I have to them is that they are so icky," sighed Lenora.

"Well, you don't have to eat any," said Lois practically. "I'll eat your share."

"Yes, you will—not!" declared Lenora emphatically. "What is this?"

Ada Collins and Virginia Harris entered with more mysterious packages.

"We bought all the butter creams Weller's had," Ada declared.

Evelyn DeLong entered with her ukulele clasped under her arm, while her roommate, Phyllis Tanner, carried a plate of fudge.

"This looks like a surprise party," said Anne. "Or is it somebody's birthday?"

"It is the birthday of a bigger and better Alpha Delta group," spoke up Connie. "We thought we would provide the refreshments on the night of our first official meeting."

"An excellent idea, too," proclaimed Lenora.

"How's the ankle, Beverly?" Connie asked.

"Fine," Beverly smiled. "How do you feel? Tired?"

"She shouldn't," cut in Kathleen. "She slept through all study period," she said laughing. "She was supposed to be studying French."

"You didn't have to tell on me," Connie murmured, joining in the laughter. "How could I keep my mind on French after we had won the championship?"

"And how can we keep our minds on something else with those cream puffs staring us in the face?" demanded Lenora.

"Perhaps we had better do away with them," suggested Phyllis.

"I'm in favor," agreed Shirley.

The cream puffs disappeared with amazing rapidity, and the butter creams and fudge were not long in following.

"We'll all be sick tomorrow," prophesied Lois.

"We can stand it," sighed Kathleen. "After all, it is in a good cause."

"And only happens once in a year," added Ada.

"I hate to think that after next month we won't be in college any more," groaned Lenora.

"You must all come back to Vernon to see us graduated," insisted Connie. "As fellow members of the Alpha Delta, it is your duty to come and see us."

"That is a date," declared Lois. "Wherever we are next June, we will come to Vernon to see the new members of our society take their last step in school life."

"Boo-hoo," murmured Lenora. "I can't bear to think of it."

"We can't stay little girls always," Beverly said slowly.

"Who said I was a little girl?" bristled Lenora.

"Nobody, darling," Rosalie soothed. "But we can't stay in school forever. I'm sure I wouldn't want to."

"Of course, after a time," Lenora agreed, "it would get monotonous."

"Not with you around," murmured Lois. "You manage to keep things moving."

"For she's a jolly good fellow," Evelyn began.

"That's wrong," cut in Lenora. "It should be, 'For we are jolly good Alphas——' "

The others joined in, and for a half hour their voices blended in songs.

"Gracious," murmured Anne, "we will have Mrs. Dennis up to investigate the noise."

"She should let us celebrate tonight," Connie declared. "You won't be here much longer."

"Will you please stop reminding us that this is our last term?" demanded Lenora loudly. "I'll be weeping on somebody's shoulder, next thing you know."

"When you feel that way it is time to adjourn," Virginia said, rising.

"Good-night, everybody—see you tomorrow." Connie and Kathleen moved to the door.

The other girls trailed behind them, and soon Shirley and Beverly were alone. Beverly, to ease her ankle, had stayed in bed ever since dinner, and now Shirley went and knelt by her side.

"Great girls," she sighed.

"Think so?" Beverly murmured.

Shirley nodded. "But I didn't always think so. I was terribly foolish, and I'm so ashamed of myself when I think of how nice they have been to me."

"Why don't you just forget all about what happened?" Beverly suggested. "The girls don't want to make you uncomfortable."

"It will always be a seven days' wonder to me why they even bothered to speak to me," Shirley said humbly. "I was such an idiot. But I'm glad I learned my lesson. I'll never be so sure of myself again."

"It had to come," Beverly smiled. "Everybody goes through a period in life when they consider themselves better than anyone else they know. Some people don't show it, and others—well, they think they are pretty good. Anyone who gets success thrown at them is bound to feel good about it."

"They needn't let it run away with them like I did," Shirley said ruefully. "There are a lot of successful people I know who aren't a bit conceited. Take you, for instance. It was a big thing when your story was chosen in the contest. Yet you didn't let it turn your head. Just being the author of that story might mean your big chance."

"I've wondered," Beverly said slowly, "didn't

Mr. Forsythe offer you a contract to go to Hollywood with him for more pictures?"

Shirley nodded confusedly. "He did, but I didn't
want to go."

"You refused?" Beverly asked incredulously.

"Yes. I wanted to finish out my term here, and
then, too, I'd rather be on the dramatic stage than
in the movies." Shirley stood up. "You must be
tired after that match this afternoon. I won't keep
you awake with my chatter."

"Please don't feel that way." Beverly caught her
friend's hand impulsively. "It is a long while since
we had one of our chats. Let's not stop."

Shirley went back to her former position, and
the two chatted for hours in the protecting darkness of their room.

CHAPTER XXII

The Senior Prom

LENORA bounced in upon Shirley and Beverly and deposited herself on the bed with a commanding:

"What are you doing?"

"Trying to write our speeches for commencement," Shirley answered. "Can you help?"

"Of course I can," Lenora said modestly. "I'm the best speech-maker in the Alpha Deltas."

"This is for commencement," Beverly laughed. "The kind of speeches you make wouldn't be proper."

"What do you mean?" Lenora demanded.

"How shall I start?" Beverly counter-questioned. "Shall I say Friends or Dear Friends? Or shall I say Faculty, Students, and Friends——"

"Gracious, haven't you gotten any farther than the salutation?" Lenora giggled. "I see where you will surely have to call in assistance."

"I'll write it all by myself," Beverly defended.

"It shouldn't be any job at all for you," Shirley chimed in. "You want to be a writer. But think of poor me. I have to have a personal message for my classmates, and what shall I say?"

"Hello!" Lois entered. "What is this? You all look so serious."

"Speeches," Shirley answered.

"One of Lenora's?" Lois paused, ready for flight.

"No," Beverly smiled, and Lois sat down thankfully.

"If I had been making a speech," Lenora said suspiciously, "would you have left right away?"

"I certainly would," Lois said candidly. "You know what I think of your speeches."

"Hm," Lenora answered. "I know, but you don't have to remind me of it. Anyway, I shall go right on speaking whenever I have anything to say."

Lois declined to comment on her friend's declaration and imparted another bit of news.

"The orchestra for the dance tonight has arrived," she said. "We saw them leave the train and depart in taxis for the country club."

"Goodness," Beverly gasped. "It is five of three, and Jim and Tommy arrive at three o'clock. I must fly to the station to meet them. Where is Anne?"

"She is already down there," Lois supplied. "She sent me along to tell you to hurry."

"And instead you don't say a word about it," commented Lenora.

"I'll see you later," Beverly called as she scattered the remnants of her speech to the four winds and departed on a run.

The ballroom of the Vernon country club had been chartered for the Senior Dance, and a special orchestra from New York had been engaged to supply the music. The girls were all excited, for it was the biggest social event of the term. Each girl had invited a boy that she knew to escort her. Anne had chosen Tommy Chandler of the Lucky Circle, and Beverly had asked Jim. Shirley's escort came from New York, and Lenora and Lois and Rosalie had each invited a boy from her home town.

Connie and Kathleen were an appreciative audience when Shirley and Beverly donned their frocks for the evening.

"You look marvelously happy tonight," Connie commented on Beverly's flushed cheeks and sparkling eyes.

"I am," she answered rapturously. "I feel as though I would burst any minute."

"Aha!" Kathleen murmured dramatically. "Methinks Jim is responsible."

"Silly," Beverly said lightly. "I'd be just as happy no matter who I was going with."

"Don't dance too much," Connie warned as Shirley and Beverly pranced to the door.

"We are going to dance until we are put out," Shirley declared.

The ballroom of the country club was decorated with the school's colors, and the lights were covered with shades composed of tiny colored crystals. Down the polished floor's wide expanse the dancers whirled, caught in a world of gayety. The shifting, delicate colors and soft, sweet music made the atmosphere enchanting.

"You are lovely tonight, Beverly," Jim whispered.

"Thank you, sir," she said lightly.

"You are like a—fairy princess just stepped from her carriage."

"And you are the fairy prince," she rejoined smilingly. "The prince on a great white horse who wins the lady's favor."

"This prince would like to steal his princess away to his castle," he murmured.

"Oh, but he can't," Beverly smiled. "He forgot his horse."

Jim laughed. "Won't you ever be serious?"

"Why should I?" Beverly asked wonderingly. "Especially on a night like this. It is so much nicer to be gay and—merry. Life makes us serious too soon, and I don't want to lose joy while I have it."

"Have—have you thought at all about what I told you on Christmas Eve?" he asked slowly.

"No," she said promptly. "I don't want to. Please, Jim, I thought you promised not to mention it again."

"I'm sorry," he said smiling. "Shall we get some punch?"

"Let's," she rejoined promptly. She had been so happy, and now she felt as if a momentary cloud had appeared on her evening. Why must she hurt Jim like this? She knew he was hurt, she could tell by his gray eyes. It wasn't fair. She couldn't help it if she didn't love him the way he wanted her to. She had thought after Christmas he would surely forget it and not mention love again, but evidently he meant to keep asking her. Why must it be so? She had not asked for his love. She wanted only her ambition. Through that she could hurt no one.

"What is the matter?" Jim asked.

"Nothing." She looked up smilingly. "I'm sorry, I was thinking."

"You were miles away," he accused laughingly.

"I promise not to do it again," she declared with a return of her former lightness.

Anne and Tommy joined them, and the four chatted for several minutes before they were again whirled away in the rhythm of the dance. After that Jim and Beverly let nothing serious creep into their conversation, but laughed and danced as gayly as though they were back in their old high-school days. Everyone there seemed bubbling over with cheer, and at the end of the evening this Senior Dance was declared the best that had ever been given.

After the dance the four friends from Renville strolled back to the Hall in the moonlight. It was June, and the evening was warm. Stars twinkled overhead like fireflies in the heavens, and moonlight sprinkled silver dust through the trees. Beverly slipped her hand within Jim's and pulled him onto another path. Tommy and Anne went on, not knowing their companions had slipped away from them.

Beverly led Jim through the college grounds behind the buildings to the woods where she liked to wander after classes. Tonight it was mysterious and silent. Only the cautious fluttering of a bird disturbed the leaves on the trees. The grass was wet with dew, and the scent of woodland flowers was in the air. Hand in hand they walked through the leaf-strewn paths, at times talking and at other times silent.

Beverly felt as if the old Jim were with her now. Always he was such a good comrade to talk and dream with, but since his return from Wyoming he had been different. Yet tonight, now, he seemed more the boy she used to know. She could talk frankly to him of things she hoped to do and to see, and he understood. It was much better this way. She did not want anything to come into either of their lives to spoil their friendship. Yet she knew, after these few minutes were over, things would go back to the way they had been. Jim would be looking for something from her that she could not give, and it was only at odd moments that she could hope to rediscover the old Jim.

Slowly they turned and made their way back to Chadwick Hall. The pillars of the Hall gleamed white against the surrounding blackness of trees and shrubbery. Tommy and Anne were sitting on the top step waiting for them.

"Aha, and where have you been?" demanded Tommy when they approached.

"We went exploring," Jim answered gayly. "We didn't think you would miss us," he added, his eyes twinkling.

"We didn't," Tommy rejoined promptly.

"All the girls have gone in already," Anne said to Beverly.

Beverly consulted her wrist watch. "Goodness, is it that late? We will have Mrs. Dennis out after us soon. We better go, too."

After bidding the boys good-night, the girls crept as silently as possible into the Hall. They had

long overstayed their allotted hours, and they had
no desire to be discovered by the mistress of the
Hall. However, they managed to reach their rooms
without being seen and to tumble into bed to
dream of the good time they had had.

CHAPTER XXIII

Senior Dinner

THE DAYS of the term were going fast now, and it would not be long before the day of days, Commencement Day, would arrive. The girls were crowding as many good times into these last hours as they could. One special affair had been planned by the girls and that was a senior dinner to be given by the class at Weller's. The whole second floor of the ice-cream saloon had been hired for the purpose, and banquet tables were erected. Lenora was chairman of the dinner committee and she reported that the girls intended to make it a most lavish affair. Favors had been bought, and flowers with which to decorate the tables. The best dinner that Weller's had on the menu would be served.

"For," she declared, "nothing is too good for the class of 19—."

"That's us," beamed Lois. "Whoops! Aren't we important?"

"Some of our members are," said Lenora. "Of course others———"

Lois cocked a stern eye in her friend's direction. "Others are—what?" she demanded. "And by 'others,' do you mean me?"

Lenora grinned cheerfully. "There you go, right away, trying to argue with me. Commencement is next week, and I refuse to argue with anyone."

Shirley shook her hand solemnly. "Such a declaration calls for congratulations. How can you resist?"

"Yes," laughed Lois. "Tell us the secret of your ponderous decision."

"I refuse," Lenora said loftily. "You had better dress, or you will be late for the dinner. I'm off now to see that everything is right side up."

"Who is going to speak?" Lois asked.

"You will be surprised," smiled Lenora.

"Not you, I hope?" Lois said suspiciously.

"Of course, I have to introduce the speakers," Lenora admitted.

"Oh, woe is me," Lois said with mock sadness and went off to dress.

The dinner hour came, and one by one the seniors arrived at Weller's. Colored paper hats were handed them at the door, and favors were before their places at the tables. A radio supplied the music for them. The tinkle of the dishes was interspersed with laughter and chatter until the dinner was eaten and Lenora, as chairman, stood up and signaled for order. Every eye was fastened on her attentively, and the girls became silent.

"At a banquet it is usually the thing to have a number of speeches," Lenora began. "The two speakers we are to have have not prepared a speech because they were not told they were going to be called upon. The members of the dinner committee thought it would be more interesting if we had speeches that were spontaneous and not prepared beforehand. Of course, the speakers will probably think differently, but we are sure whatever they will say will be interesting.

"The first young lady I am going to call upon is one who, though still in college, has had a taste of success in the career she has chosen for her life after commencement. I refer to our valedictorian—Miss Shirley Parker."

To the accompaniment of a burst of applause Shirley rose to her feet. She thanked them almost shyly. It was a different Shirley, this who spoke to her classmates. Some of her listeners had not spoken to her since the time when she had been overwhelmed by her own success, and now they were surprised at the change in her. No longer was she the arrogant girl who had been the star in the moving picture.

Beverly, sitting next to Lenora, looked at the latter smilingly. "It was fine of you, Lenora, to call on Shirley."

Lenora smiled confusedly. "I wanted the other girls to see how different she is now. All her old friends will come back after this."

"She has you to thank for it," Beverly murmured.

"Nonsense," Lenora returned gruffly, but she was nevertheless pleased.

Shirley spoke simply and humorously, and the girls felt their hearts warming to her. When she sat down abruptly, applause poured forth. If anyone had looked closely enough, they might have seen the joyous tears in Shirley's eyes. She knew once more the joy of being loved and respected by many friends.

Lenora rose and demanded order again. "And now we have another member of our class—a very dear member. You all know her and love her for the wonderful girl she is. I'm sure we couldn't graduate properly without a word from our president to go with us. Miss Beverly Gray——"

Beverly rose, the color in her cheeks, and her eyes dancing. After a few humorous remarks on the injustice of calling upon anyone to make a speech so unexpectedly, Beverly became serious.

"I want to say that it has been a real pleasure

to be associated with each and every one of you," she said slowly, "and I wish you all well in the future. We have had many enjoyable times together, and I know that after we leave Vernon more good times are in store. This is probably the last time we shall all meet as students to enjoy ourselves together, but soon we shall have another responsibility: that which goes with being members of the alumnae of the college. Next week we graduate. Many of us, in fact all of us, have looked forward to the time when we shall receive our diploma. It means many things, but most of all it means separation.

"When we leave Vernon we shall go on to different positions and live different lives. Many of you will go out into the world to earn your own living, and you will meet shadows. The way will prove thorny and rough to some, and yet the future, whether for honor or dishonor, rests in our own hands. With a high aim, firm purpose, and unselfish ambition, we can make of our lives what we will.

"I know you, as graduates of Vernon, will keep with you the ideals and traditions that you have gathered here, and I wish for you all the haven of success which we all seek."

CHAPTER XXIV

Commencement

COMMENCEMENT DAY dawned gloriously bright and sunshiny, as though to do its part to drown out the dark sorrows of good-byes. With a swelling of pride and sinking of heart the girls had come finally to their goal—the last of many college days. During their four terms they had shared pleasures and sorrows, and the friendships that had been made would remain unchanged in defeat or success. Now, with their last few hours at Vernon ahead of them, they were drawn together in steadfast loyalty as never before.

The hotels in Vernon were overflowing with parents, friends, and relatives of the graduates who had journeyed to see this class of young people take the last important step of their school life.

The six Alphas were gathered for one final last moment as students in Beverly's and Shirley's room.

"I don't want to graduate," wailed Lenora as she placed her cap at a more rakish angle.

"At last we agree on something," sighed Lois. "They should let us be seniors for two years."

"We're grown up now," Beverly said smiling. "We can't stay in school forever, and we shouldn't expect to. We have to make way for new students."

"Maybe we can come back as freshmen next term," suggested Lenora brightly.

"They are glad to get rid of you now," Lois teased. "They wouldn't let you in for another four years."

"It is time to go," Shirley advised.

"Yes, we better hurry," admonished Anne and Rosalie.

Beverly regarded each of her friends with bright eyes. "Well, girls, we've come to the end of Senior Road. In another few hours we shall be on our own to make what we can of our lives."

"It will help to know that at least this six will always stand ready to help one another," Lenora said, for once in her four years, seriously. "If any one of us ever needs help we will call upon our friends, and the Alphas will always answer the call."

"Right you are," agreed Lois promptly. "The

Alpha Deltas were formed not to last only for as long as our college life, but for always."

"Let's plan a day for our next meeting," Shirley suggested. "I would like to have you all in New York."

"But we promised to come to Vernon to see the other members of the Alpha Deltas graduated next June," reminded Anne.

"So we did," Shirley agreed.

"Then, though we go to the ends of the earth, as the poets say, we shall come to Vernon next June," declared Lenora.

"You are right again," said Lois. "Gracious, now I know it is a special day. I have agreed with Lenora twice in the last fifteen minutes!"

"We better go, or we will have the Dean coming for us," declared Rosalie.

The class members were to gather in the gymnasium and from there march to the chapel where the graduation exercises would be held. Beverly, as president, and Shirley, as valedictorian, walked at the head of the long line of students. The girls looked curiously stately and dignified in their caps and gowns. The chapel was crowded, and as they marched down the aisle Beverly sent a smile across to her parents that set their hearts glowing with pride. Jim and Tommy, too, were on hand to see the big event.

Beverly looked about the old chapel with loving eyes. She had indeed come to the end of Senior Road. She had been living in a world of girlish dreams and troubles, but now all that was past. Her girlhood was almost over, and she was going out onto the road of life to seek her place. She had to find her work and to do it gladly and whole-heartedly. It might not be easy, for the pathway of life is strewn with pitfalls and temptations, but she would do her best. When she found her work in life she would do it nobly and truly.

The door to the future was swinging wide, and she was about to step through to meet the biggest adventure of all. She would take with her memories of the girls and scenes she had known. She would take with her the high ideals, good sportsmanship, clear thinking, and the courage that had grown to be a part of her daily life here at Vernon. Of course, it was hard to leave the old scenes and friends, but she welcomed this new adventure. It would bring her new scenes and contacts with new and strange people. Now she could devote herself to her ambition, and she did not propose to relin-quish her hold on that ambition until it had been realized. She was going to forge ahead to success and make her parents and her friends proud of her. She was determined to play her part in the great scheme of life to the best of her ability.

The exercises were over, and the students filed out to receive the congratulations of their friends.

"My word, but you look grown up in that cap and gown," Jim declared, shaking hands with her.

She laughed. "But I'm not really. Underneath it I'm just the same as I always was."

"We're glad of that," her mother said fondly. "We don't want you to grow away from us."

"I shan't ever," Beverly declared firmly.

"Now that you have your sheepskins," Tommy said laughingly, "what are you going to do with them?"

"Frame them," Anne said promptly, "and hang them on our wall as a reminder of our four years here."

"Just think," Tommy grinned, "four years to get a sheet of paper."

"It isn't the paper that counts," Beverly said, "it is the thought behind it. They have been four of our happiest years."

"Indeed they have," Anne agreed.

"I imagine you will be able to find compensations," Tommy said with such an ardent glance at Anne that again Beverly wondered if there was anything between them.

Late that night, after they had said good-night to the other Alpha members, Shirley and Beverly

stood looking out at the ivy-covered college buildings. The moonlight made the buildings look black
and solid as they stood like silent guardians of the
treasure of learning. The spire of the chapel
reached up into the sky like a hand reaching for
the twinkling stars. Each foot of campus, and each
austere building, held a place in their hearts.

"And tomorrow we shall leave it all," Shirley
said slowly. "Are you happy?"

"Yes," Beverly admitted. "For all that I hate to
leave, and it will be hard, yet I'm glad that at last
I'm going to start to really make my own place."

"How will you do it?" Shirley asked.

"I don't know," Beverly admitted. "I have always wanted to be a reporter on a newspaper, but
Mother doesn't want me to go to New York, and
there is no paper in Renville. That is, none to speak
of. I expect I shall devote my time to stories. I
might even try to write a play sometime. What
shall you do?"

"Mother is still opposed to my becoming an
actress," Shirley sighed. "But I shall go right ahead
with my plans all the same," she declared with a
toss of her head. "Do you remember the man who
came to see me after we gave the freshman production of *Romeo and Juliet?*"

"Yes. His name was—Crandall, wasn't it?" Beverly said.

"Andrew T. Crandall," Shirley confirmed. "Remember, I promised to go and see him after graduation, and he said he might give me a part in his show."

"I remember," Beverly said. "That summer he was putting on *Romeo and Juliet,* and he wanted you to go with him and play the part of Juliet."

"Yes. Well, I shall go to him as soon as I land in New York," Shirley said determinedly. "I know Mother will be angry, but I'm going anyway. I'm not going in for society like she wants me to do. I don't want to go to endless teas and meet boresome people and have to be nice to them whether I like them or not. I want to be an actress, and I'm going to be one!"

"Three cheers for you," Beverly applauded. "I wonder what the rest of the girls will do?"

Shirley laughed. "Lenora declares it is her sole intention to do nothing but enjoy herself. Lois wants to sketch. She has real talent, too. Did she show you the picture she drew of the Hall the other day?"

"No," Beverly said in surprise. "I never knew Lois had such an ambition. Why has she kept it a secret?"

"Because Lenora would tease her about it," Shirley smiled. "Those two are at continual war, you know—good-naturedly, of course. All the same, Lois doesn't want her lone talent, as she calls it, jeered at by Lenora."

"But Lenora doesn't mean anything by her teasing," Beverly said, laughing. "It seems to me Lois does plenty of it herself."

"Of course she does," Shirley agreed, "and Lenora would understand about her sketching, but Lois insists she doesn't want to tell anyone. She wouldn't have told me, but I caught her at it."

"What about Rosalie and Anne?" Beverly wondered.

"It seems to me that they are the two ladies in our group," Shirley smiled. "They are the kind who should devote themselves to society—they are so gracious and contented. They will get along at whatever they try, don't you think?"

"I believe they will," Beverly agreed. "Rosalie told me she would like to go to a conservatory and continue her music. Who knows?—we might have a famous concert pianist in our group some day."

"Ho—hum," Shirley yawned prodigiously. "As much as I hate to admit it, I'm getting sleepy. It has been a busy day."

"What did your parents think of Vernon?" Beverly asked.

"Father thought it was splendid," Shirley said

smiling. "But you know Mother. Ever the society woman! If the doors had had gold doorknobs and the buildings diamond-studded window sills, Mother would have liked it more. As it was, she deemed it quite nice and let it go at that."

CHAPTER XXV

Auld Lang Syne

"SHOULD auld acquaintance be forgot," bellowed Boyd Marshall as he picked out the notes of the melody with one finger on the piano.

"May I ask what you are doing?" inquired Gordon, seating himself at Boyd's side on the piano bench.

"Of course, I'm singing," Boyd replied with dignity.

Gordon shook his head sorrowfully. "My dear fellow, you are laboring under a terrible hallucination. I would call it groaning——"

Boyd frowned on him. "Do you know what groaning is? It is a low, deep sound uttered in pain or sorrow. And as I am not in pain and have no overwhelming sorrow——"

"I still say it is groaning," declared Gordon.

Boyd moved so swiftly that before Gordon knew what was happening he had slid from the piano bench to the floor.

"There, let that be a lesson to you!" Boyd said triumphantly. "I allow no one to make sarcastic remarks about my singing."

"Groaning," Gordon insisted and beat a hasty retreat to the dining room.

Barbara and Joan were setting the table under the supervision of Anne and Tommy. Beverly was in the kitchen with Jim, dishing out ice cream.

"I've got an offer of a job in South America," Jim said abruptly as he came back from delivering two dishes to the dining-room table.

"Jim, that's marvelous!" Beverly declared. "What is it, another bridge?"

"A canal of some sort," Jim answered unenthusiastically. "It will take about eight months or a year."

"Aren't you thrilled?" Beverly asked smiling. "Things seem to be coming your way."

"Oh, I like the work all right," Jim agreed slowly. "But it will mean that I won't see you for a long time."

Beverly paused, the ice-cream spoon suspended in midair. "Are you still thinking of—that, Jim?"

He nodded.

"I wish you would forget it, truly I do," she said earnestly. "I don't want things like that for us— not yet, anyway."

"Sometime?" he asked eagerly.

"Maybe," she answered, the color in her cheeks. "But I want to write for a while. If I don't get a chance to do some of the things I want to do, I would always be restless. I would always think there was something I missed."

"I wouldn't interfere with your writing," he said hastily.

"But it wouldn't be the same," she urged. "You see what I mean, don't you?" she asked pleadingly.

"I see," he said slowly. He grinned cheerfully. "The ice cream will be melted if we don't hurry."

"We thought you had decided to eat it all yourselves," Boyd declared when they appeared in the dining room.

"It is what you deserve," Gordon said wickedly, "after punishing us with such cruel music."

"Listen to him," wailed Boyd. "He doesn't appreciate good music. My friend, I play just like Chopin or any great player."

"Oh-ho, listen to him," chortled Gordon. "Why do you rate yourself with such well known men? Tell me the secret of your success," he begged.

"I use both hands," retorted Boyd.

At that ponderous remark Gordon choked on his piece of cake and had to be pounded heartily on the back. When he regained his breath he made a lurch for Boyd, and a scrimmage might have resulted had not the others interfered and restored peace.

"Tsk, tsk," said Gordon, with a groan. "Such a joke!"

"By the way," Beverly interrupted, "Anne told me she had something to announce. What is it?"

Anne looked appealingly at Tommy, and he smiled at them all.

"Anne has promised to marry me," he said simply.

For an instant there was silence. The surprise had been complete. Then such an uproar of congratulations and handshaking and kissing that ensued.

"This is why you have been so happy ever since Christmas," Beverly accused fondly.

Anne nodded smilingly. "We—we decided then, but we wanted to wait for a while before we told anyone. We weren't to be married until next spring, but——"

"I have to go West on a business trip, and I want Anne to come with me," finished Tommy.

"Now we are really grown up," sighed Barbara. "All through with college and Anne and Tommy getting married! I can't believe it."

"That's the way I feel," Tommy said with a glance at Anne. "I hope I don't wake up and find it all a dream."

Boyd promptly pinched him, and at Tommy's howl explained, "I was merely assuring you that it isn't a dream."

"When is the big affair to be?" Joan asked.

"In three weeks," Anne answered. "It won't be a big ceremony, because we don't want much fuss. Immediately afterward we shall board the train——"

"For the Golden West," supplied Boyd. "Ah, love is grand!"

"Isn't it, though?" mimicked Gordon, laying a heavy hand on Boyd's collar. "Now I am going to pay you for that terrible joke about Chopin."

"Owwww, help!" Boyd yelled as Gordon propelled him through the front door.

"There, that will teach him a lesson!" Gordon declared dusting himself off as he reappeared in the dining room.

"Methinks I hear supplications for deliverance," murmured Joan.

"He will wear out the doorbell," declared Barbara, as the bell pealed loudly.

"Tell him to stop," begged Joan.

"I'll stop him," Gordon said grimly and went to the door.

As soon as Gordon disappeared from the dining room, Boyd stuck his head in from the kitchen.

"Good-evening, everyone. Lovely weather we are having, isn't it? Beverly, may I sit by you?"

"How did you do it?" Tommy demanded.

"A pin stuck in the button of the bell creates the illusion that someone is at the door, while that someone may be entering by the back door," explained Boyd. He looked up with a wide grin as Gordon reëntered. "Good-evening, Gordon. Are you just arriving?"

Gordon sank back in his seat with a murmured, "What's the use?"

"That is what I always say," beamed Boyd. "What is the use of worrying?"

The jollity kept up far into the night with laughter and singing that set the house to echoing. When her hilarious guests had departed and the last good-night had been said, Beverly went to her room and knelt by the open window.

The night was warm, and the sky looked like a soft blanket studded with diamond stars. The scent of honeysuckle was wafted on the breeze. The birds had all gone to their nests in the trees in the garden, and the world below was silent. Beverly rested her chin on her folded arms and stared out into the night with retrospective eyes.

Barbara had said that at last they were grown up. Anne and Tommy were about to join hands and go the rest of their way in life together. The two with whom she had romped and played through school days were to take their next important step side by side. They were to keep the precious gift that had come to them and cherish it through all the years to come.

Looking up at the stars Beverly wondered what the future held in store for her. Whether she would find the exciting things which she craved. Whether she would ever travel and see the things that fascinated her.

Three weeks later the little church on the hill was the scene of the simple but impressive ceremony that joined the two young people together for all time. All the Alpha Deltas had journeyed to Renville from their homes to see their member take such an important step. All the Lucky Circle had turned out, and with them most of the young people in Renville, for both Tommy and Anne were popular in their home town.

Anne had decided on having only one attendant, and the girls were all satisfied when her choice fell on Beverly. As for that young lady, she was in seventh heaven of delight. Tommy had chosen Jim for his best man, and as the four left the church, it was hard to tell which couple was the handsomer.

The reception at the home of the bride was for

merely her closest friends—the Alpha Deltas and the Lucky Circle. The newly-weds declared they couldn't start off on their honeymoon without the good wishes of their friends. The party all escorted Anne and Tommy to the station, and there was the usual bustle of last good-byes.

The two climbed aboard the train, and as it chugged slowly out of the station Boyd murmured reflectively:

"And so they were married and lived happily ever after."

"Just like a fairy story," added Lenora.

"It was a beautiful wedding " sighed Rosalie.

"Tell me, why did some of the women cry?" demanded Gordon.

"Because they were happy," answered Joan.

"But if one is happy there is nothing to cry about," insisted Boyd.

"Oh, you wouldn't understand," declared Barbara.

"I understand one thing," Boyd grinned, "I'm hungry."

"After all you've eaten?" gasped Jim.

"Shucks," murmured Boyd. "I didn't eat much."

"Oh, no," teased Gordon. "I'll bet some of the guests thought you were a baby elephant in disguise."

"I'm insulted," declared Boyd loftily.

The Lucky Circle departed to their homes—that is, all but Beverly. The Alpha Delta girls were to board their train in a few minutes to take them back to their homes, and Beverly had elected to stay at the station until they were gone.

"Well," Lois sighed, "Anne is the first one of our group to take the fatal step."

"I wonder who will be next?" Connie Elwood murmured, smiling on them.

"Not me!" declared Lenora with such vigor that the rest laughed. "Me for the life of a sailor," she sang saucily.

"Are you going to join the navy?" demanded Lois.

Lenora laughed. "Of course not, but I'm going to work on their principles—you know, a girl in every port. My motto is a boy in every town."

"Aha! A female Bluebeard!" declaimed Lois.

"Goodness," Lenora said, "I don't behead people."

"No," teased Lois, "you talk them to death. It is the same thing."

"Boo-hoo," wailed Lenora. "You don't appreciate me. Some day you will be sorry you said mean things to me. Wait until I'm rich and famous—I won't even look at you."

"What is going to make you famous?" jeered Lois.

"Somebody might die and leave me a fortune," continued Lenora. "Then you will be sorry you weren't nice to me."

"We've been nice to you," Shirley smiled. "What do we get?"

"A lollypop for each one," promised Lenora laughingly.

"Is that all?" Beverly sighed.

"It isn't worth the effort," declared Lois.

The train whistle sounded as the black giant rounded the bend above the town.

"Ah, our chariot approacheth," murmured Lenora. "Good-bye, everybody."

"If any of you come to New York in your travels, be sure to look me up," begged Shirley. "I know I shall probably waste away in boredom because I shall miss your nonsense."

"At last somebody will miss me," beamed Lenora. "My friend, I shall come to see you—when I visit New York," she added.

"That is a promise," Shirley agreed.

"If any of you want to, you are welcome to come and spend the summer with me," offered Beverly. "I know I shall be lonesome, too."

"It isn't a case of wanting to," said Lois. "It is a case of can we? I have to go home and take charge of my kid sister while my parents go off to the mountain for a week. Then we shall probably go to the seashore."

"Just the same," Beverly said, "if any of you have the chance, come to Renville to see me."

Let us here take leave of the Alpha Delta girls and their friends for a while. Those who have learned to look upon Beverly and the others as friends will find new adventures in *Beverly Gray's Career*, in which we learn to what the girls devoted themselves after college days. We shall, too, follow Beverly's adventures as she wins a place for herself as a reporter on a leading newspaper.

THE END